I0545998

Where Seagulls Sleep

Where Seagulls Sleep

Virginia Young

Riverhaven Books
www.RiverhavenBooks.com

Where Seagulls Sleep is a work of fiction. While some of the settings in Rhode Island are actual, any similarity regarding names, characters, or incidents is entirely coincidental.

Copyright© 2014 by Virginia Young

All rights reserved.

Published in the United States by Riverhaven Books, www.RiverhavenBooks.com

ISBN : 978-1-937588-35-9

Printed in the United States of America by Country Press, Lakeville, Massachusetts

Designed and Edited by Stephanie Lynn Blackman Whitman, MA

This book is written in memory of all those who get lost in the world and have no one to search for them.

*With thanks
to my husband, Ed,
for journeying with me to our favorite places
as well as for his input on what I write,
to my daughter, Stephanie,
for her time, effort, and support,
and to my beloved creatures and grandchildren
who inspire me to find the joy in each day.*

Also by Virginia Young

Out of the Blue
A romance set in Massachusetts

The Birthday Gift
A romance set in Connecticut

Sleepless Tides
A romance set in Maine

Winter Waltz
A romance set in Vermont

By a Thread
A contemporary novel

Find Me
A collection of short stories and poetry

A Family of Strangers
A romantic suspense set in Canada and New Hampshire

I Call Your Name
A romantic suspense set on Martha's Vineyard

Nocturnal
A young adult novel

Chapter One

The only window at the front of her rented cottage was small and draped in what Catherine thought of as old-lady lace. She stood there for the tenth time that day, pulling the intricate fabric aside to peer out at the cottages across the street. Narrow slivers of space between each colorful dwelling offered a tease-view of the sea and surf.

Trini was missing. She was known to stay at the beach for prolonged periods. It was important for Catherine to watch every move – to explore every sound of a car door opening and closing, to take note of anyone new and different.

It was late afternoon and at least the twentieth time that day Catherine had pulled the curtain aside when she saw him. He was getting out of his car parked on a mix of gravel and grass directly in front of the small blue cottage across from her own of faded yellow. He was tall and slim and had an air of mystery about him with black slacks, black shirt; his hair equally as dark. She watched him with interest. He had a definite confidence in his stride as he moved those long legs toward the front door of the cottage. He inserted a key, then turned and looked directly at Catherine's place. Her eyes caught a small patch of white at his throat. *A minister? A priest?*

Startled by his directed stare toward her, she let go of the curtain and backed away. A corner of the lace became entangled on itself and left a length of glass bare. His eyes seemed fastened to that spot, to the movement. Could he know Trini? Could he be harboring her from harm?

Catherine leaned back against the nautical patterned wall next to the window and took a deep breath. Where could Trini be, she wondered, as she edged forward and looked through the window. He was gone, but there was something left in his wake, something about the intensity reflected on his handsome face. Catherine walked to a chair and sat down. Her feelings were puzzling; why, she wondered, would she be attracted to a stranger, someone who could be potentially dangerous. After all, she reasoned, his clothing might serve as a disguise. He could be one of the ruthless thugs rumored to be involved with her young half-sister.

As the day began to lose light, Catherine rubbed her neck and walked to the small kitchen equipped with an apartment-sized refrigerator and a two-burner stovetop. No oven, no microwave. She boiled water in a small pan and made tea. She thought about the job she'd forfeited when she'd been told to give up on the investigation. She'd liked being a police officer, following in her father's footsteps. But finding Trini was not something she could do without leaving her job. The orders were there – let it go. She could not abide by that demand. Finding her drug-involved sister was front and center.

Catherine looked at the photo. Trini had just the hint of a smile on her lips, as if someone told her to appear happy but she gave them only a fraction of what they asked. Her blonde hair was in a single braid hung over her left shoulder spilling onto her chest. She looked so young. She was twenty-two, but in this image, she looked no more than a teenager.

Catherine walked back toward the front window carrying her tea. As she positioned herself at the panel of lace, she could see that the tall, slim man, who had walked into the cottage in black, was now wearing chino pants and a light blue shirt, its long sleeves rolled back to his elbows. She watched him. He took keys from his trouser pocket and, before opening the car door, he glanced briefly toward Catherine's cottage then disappeared into his vehicle. Catherine stepped back as he maneuvered the car onto the narrow beach road and drove slowly away.

There was a feeling that swept over her – as if this man was going to play a part in her life. She found it unsettling to think what part that might be. He could be hazardous. And yet something propelled her to think perhaps he wasn't. She didn't know. What she wanted to know was how to find Trini.

Catherine walked back toward the kitchen and thought about food. With the kitchen window propped open using a slim length of wood, she could smell the salt air and the occasional waft of barbequed burgers and roasted corn. She'd had nothing more than a banana and tea all day. The café down the street might offer a double source: food and information could come in a set.

With a light sweater over her thin blouse, Catherine walked past several other cottages where hotdogs were being grilled and beer was being swilled, as if part of a contest. It was a honky-tonk area, not a place she would choose for a vacation rental. But, she reminded herself as she nodded hello to the friendly inhabitants she passed, this was not a vacation. This was serious business. Find Trini before she was found by two men who seemed determined to steal her away. Why? What was this about? Catherine wanted desperately to find her, to protect her.

At the café, the heavy aroma of beer mixed with fried food caused her to take shallow breaths. She began to wonder if she'd made the right decision about getting something to eat there in order to have questions answered. She needed to blend in; she needed to be discreet.

At the bar, she ordered a Diet Coke and a plate of nachos from the scant menu. She sat down on a stool and looked around. The place was alive with rough-looking heavy drinkers and noise, voices competing with loud music. It was only moments before a barbaric looking man in his mid-forties sat down beside her, his tattooed arms bare where sleeves had been ruthlessly severed at the shoulder. She felt his eyes on her as she sipped her Coke and waited for the nachos.

"I saw you in here a couple of nights ago," he said. "I was about to introduce myself when you left. The name's Roy," he declared as he extended a thick hand toward Catherine.

Reluctantly, she looked at him and shook his hand.

"Got a name?" he asked with a toothy smile.

"Catherine," she said as nachos were placed before her.

"You got good taste there, Catherine. The nachos here are the best. So, you new around here?"

Catherine placed a dripping nacho in her mouth,

sipped Coke to quiet the hot sauce and replied, "I'm here for a couple of weeks."

"Vacation time?" he asked as he ordered a beer.

Catherine picked at the nachos, trying to avoid the hot peppers and nodded. "Yes, I thought I'd spend some time at the sea."

Roy laughed. "You sure can tell when someone's a lady. The way you talk, you know? 'Time at the sea' – that's classy. Most people around here just say they're down at the beach."

Catherine used a stiff paper napkin to pat at her lips and wipe grease from her fingertips. "Well, I'm looking for someone," she said. "She's in her early twenties, blonde hair, wears it in a braid. You haven't seen anyone like that, have you?"

Her rugged companion shook his head. "Nope, just got here a few days ago. I get around, haven't been here for years. Thought I'd check this place out again."

This, Catherine understood, was a go no-where conversation and the nachos were terrible. She paid her bill, said a pleasant good-bye to her companion, and left.

Walking back to the cottage, she took in every possible person and place along the way. People there seemed happy, as if it was their idea of a get-a-way. Loud music, liquor and fast food – none of it appealed to Catherine. And then she saw him drive past her and pull into his driveway. She slowed her pace to watch as he parked the car, locked it and walked to the cottage door. He went in and turned on a light, closing the door behind him. Catherine moved slowly toward her own front door, opened it with a tarnished key and stepped inside. What, she wondered, was a man like him doing in a place like this? He had an air of class, of confidence. He wasn't at all like anyone she'd encountered on the strip.

Catherine slipped out of her sweater and looked around. The place was small and dismal, nothing more than a shelter. She was tired and tense. She wanted to find Trini.

She walked to the sofa, its floral fabric worn and faded. No doubt this piece of furniture had accommodated many summer visitors over the years. She touched a corner of one arm and then walked to a wooden rocking chair where she sat down in semi-darkness. Catherine looked up at the gray ceiling and scanned the room. It wasn't much, but she could envision families coming in from the beach with sandy feet and wet bathing suits, laughing, the way a family should when vacationing together.

But Trini was never far from her thoughts. The girl was young, no doubt impressionable, and a suspected user of cocaine. Where was she? How did an attractive blonde hide so effectively?

Catherine stood and paced the small living room. She walked again to the window, her eyes on the cottage across the street. The car was there, at least one light was on, and she wondered: What does a man who drives his kind of car, sensible, who dresses nicely when not in his clerical clothing, find appealing about staying in that small cottage? She surmised that his circumstances might not be so different from her own. She smiled and looked down at her sandaled feet. He could wonder the same thing about her, that is, if he knew she existed.

Catherine walked to the kitchen, boiled water, scrubbed a dingy cup and made tea. She walked back to the front room of the three-room abode and glanced outside at the couples walking by. Some were hand in hand, others held bottles of beer in one hand, a cigarette in the other. This was a terrible place. She hated the thought of her sister finding solace in this environment. What kind of life did Trini have if this was her idea of a break? Catherine took a deep breath and looked out through the lace curtain at a few glaring streetlights and a darkened sky. As she allowed her eyes to dart from person to person, she became aware of movement at the cottage door across the street. There he was again – those long legs striding away from the door and toward his car. He unlocked it, took something small from the back seat area, then climbed into the vehicle, backed out of the driveway and pulled away. Catherine backed up just a foot or two from the window and, without any idea why, felt a sense of loss at his going.

There for just over one week, Catherine already felt bored with the place. No TV, no radio, but she had her phone to keep up with the news and a few friends. Mostly she listened and observed. As inconspicuously as possible, she searched for any sign of Trini or someone who might know her. The lack of her own activity and heightened sense of concern, always on edge, gave her an anxious demeanor and a deep measure of loneliness. Didn't anyone else care that Trini was missing?

Over the next two days, Catherine slept in spurts and drank tea or coffee. She watched the cottage across the street, half-afraid that her attraction to that man was somehow inappropriate. Every time she saw him, she felt a surge of adrenalin rush to her chest and she was reminded that he could mean danger. Not just for her, but for Trini.

On her tenth day at the cottage, Catherine went to her car and drove three miles away, up toward the wealthy homes along the beach, away from the honky-tonk music and distracting lights. She found a length of grass and a walkway down four steps to the sand and rocks. Stepping carefully onto a length of flat stone, she found a seat where the surf spray teased at but didn't quite reach her toes. It was soothing. It was what she needed. The only thing missing was a cup of hot coffee; next time.

"Nice, isn't it?" the male voice said, startling Catherine to the point that she nearly lost her balance on the narrow slice of granite.

She turned and was stunned as she stared into the dark eyes of her cottage neighbor from across the street. She said nothing but felt her heart pounding. Had he followed her?

"Sorry, did I frighten you?" he asked as he moved closer and sat down a crevice and five feet away.

"A little," she said.

"I come here every day," he said. "I don't think I could ever get tired of this."

Catherine looked at him. With his thick black hair and brown eyes, the tan sweater and jeans, he could have stepped out of a men's magazine. Thinking there was little sense in lying, she admitted she'd seen him.

"You're in the blue cottage across from me," she

said.

"Right," he replied.

So he'd noticed her. Catherine swallowed and turned her eyes to the sea.

"Are you enjoying your vacation?" he asked.

Catherine looked down at her white sandals and wished she had noticed that her red toenails needed a touch-up. "It's okay," she said. "What about you?"

"I," he said, "am not completely on vacation; I am a fraud."

Catherine didn't conceal her surprise as she turned to face him. "What?"

He laughed as he drew up his outstretched legs so that his knees faced the sky. "I'm hiding. The name's Luke Renoir, by the way."

"Renoir? As in the French painter?"

Luke smiled. "Same name, same spelling, not the same talent. I'm afraid the only thing I ever painted was a red wheelbarrow and I did that poorly. It peeled shortly after and needed to be scraped and re-done. Not fun."

His face seemed kind. Could she be wrong about that?

"I'm Catherine," she said.

They were too far apart to shake hands, but they acknowledged one another with slight nods and pleasant smiles. A period of silence followed as they each gazed out to the white-capped green sea of the Rhode Island coast.

"What did you mean about being a fraud?" Catherine asked.

Luke looked at her. "Just that I'm not what I seem,

I suppose."

Catherine looked away and then back at him. What was the risk here? He'd given her a lead, why shouldn't she follow it?

"I'm not sure I understand," she said, "but you're certainly not obliged to explain."

Luke was quiet, his heavily lashed eyes squinting against the glare of the sun on the surf. Seagulls swooped down, circled around, then flew up and gracefully landed on rocks close to the water below them.

"Did you ever wonder where seagulls sleep?" he asked.

Catherine watched the white and gray gulls then looked at her companion.

"I guess I haven't given it much thought. Where do they go at night?"

"I'm not sure anyone knows. I've asked experts. At dusk, they just sort of disappear. The theory presented to me by the author of a book on sea life is that they hunker down in rocks away from night winds. All feathered creatures have difficulty when gusts tug at their wings. Still, it's a mystery where they actually button down to rest."

Catherine's eyes went back to the gulls; she could see that they were struggling to stand erect with the wind and spray of the surf working against them.

"Have you been here on these rocks before?" he asked.

Catherine shook her head. "No. I've driven past, but I haven't stopped until today."

"Do you know the area?"

"Not really," Catherine admitted.

After a few moments of silence Luke said, "May I ask what you do with yourself in that little cottage? And what you do to occupy your time and earn a living?"

"No," she said. Then realizing how abrupt she'd been, she turned to him and apologized. "I don't mean to be evasive, it's hard to explain. What brought you to that little cottage you're staying in?"

Luke smiled. "Hiding, I guess. You know, I think we're complicated. Let's give ourselves a little time before we discuss our deep, dark secrets. What if I brought us two cups of hot chocolate right here tomorrow, same time, eleven o'clock?"

"Make it coffee with cream and two sugars and you have a deal," she said.

When he stood, he smiled as he turned and then walked away, carefully choosing his steps. She watched him disappear over rocks, the cement wall and then where he must have parked; Catherine turned back toward the sea. After a few moments, she stood and made her way toward the car, stepping over some narrow and some wide spaces where shells and tiny stones had gathered. 'Hiding' he'd said - like the shells and sea-stones between the large rock formations – he was interesting.

Catherine reached her car and found that Luke was gone. She liked him. At least she felt drawn to him with no idea why, other than the fact that he was probably the best-looking man she had ever seen. She slid into the driver's seat and sat there for a while wondering what to do next. She had so hoped that by staying at the beach strip she would simply catch a glimpse of Trini.

Nothing, there had been no sign of her or anyone remotely like her.

Catherine started the car's engine and put the gears into reverse. She carefully backed up to avoid any boulders, then pulled forward and drove toward the cottage.

Inside the small structure, she stood with her back to the door. It was damp and chilly for mid-July, with tourists coming and going. How would this affect her efforts to find Trini? The constant change in faces made the search an on-going challenge.

Catherine walked to the bedroom where a small selection of clothing remained in her suitcase. The place hadn't looked clean; she had no wish to hang her blouses and other clothing in the small closet. Changing her clothes, she selected a pale blue cardigan and slipped it on over a t-shirt.

The sparse conversation with the very alluring Luke Renoir gave her reason to wonder: What was he concealing? He'd admitted to being 'a fraud', and there was that glimpse of white at his gorgeous throat when she first saw him wearing all black.

"Just my luck," she whispered to the ceiling. "I finally meet a guy who interests me and he's given his heart and soul to Father, Son and Holy Ghost." Catherine checked her watch. It was just after one in the afternoon. She walked to the window and looked at the empty driveway in front of the blue cottage across the street. She pouted then thought about what to do next.

As a police officer for three years, she'd been assigned to a cruiser. She'd hoped to eventually become a detective, and now she was simply unemployed.

Persisting in her decision to search for her sister had caused a rift between her and the chief. She had no experience in searching for the missing, and authority to do so had been harshly denied. She had no one to count on but herself.

Deciding that she couldn't cope with hour after hour of being in the cottage peering out through the small window, Catherine grabbed her purse, locked the door and left. She stood by her car but instead decided to walk. Maybe she could catch a glimpse of Trini – maybe she could show her picture around again. It was disheartening. She needed to be careful, not to raise suspicion about what she was doing and who she was, and yet, she had no choice but to make discreet inquiries. Trini seemed innocent, yet she did not exist in an innocent world.

She had been lured into feeling accepted and being given a place to live. Who deserved the finger of blame for this young woman's self-destructive life? Catherine felt responsible. Why didn't anyone else? And who were the two men looking for her? If Catherine had even a hint about where her sister was, it would need to be kept under wraps so that word would not travel to the men, who for whatever reason, were also in search of Trini.

Catherine walked toward the cafés and general activity of the strip. She did not see, among the throngs of people, anything that resembled a family. It seemed that there were hundreds of disconnected people trying to blend with one another. There were motorcycles, inexpensive cars, profanity, and lots of beer and hotdogs. It wasn't how Catherine had grown up or spent her youth. Why was this okay for her sister? Catherine wanted to cry. She looked at the faces of forlorn people trying to mend their woes with alcohol and rough talk. She wanted to find Trini and get her out of this place.

At an open bar, Catherine saw a pile of oranges, lemons and limes. She leaned toward the bartender and asked if she could purchase a few oranges. He grinned and said that she could. Further down the colorful strip, Catherine saw a vendor selling baked potatoes wrapped in foil. She bought two, placed them inside her purse with the oranges and walked on. Always vigilant, Catherine searched the street for a wholesome looking blonde with a braid hanging to the side. She'd been told that Trini always wore her hair that way, no matter what she was doing.

At a roadside stand, Catherine bought herself a large iced coffee and then remembered that she had an eleven o'clock date with Luke Renoir for the next morning. She could not figure out why that appointment on the rocks gave her a feeling of hope. The man had great appeal, not just in his outstandingly good looks, but also in his demeanor. There was a gentleness, almost an innocence, that Catherine found both puzzling and soothing.

Reversing her half-mile walk, Catherine turned toward the cottage. It was approaching five in the afternoon; she was tired and getting hungry. Back at the cottage, she wished she had a microwave to heat the potatoes, but there was none. She unwrapped one and cut it into four sections. She ate half of it and then peeled and ate an orange as she finished the iced coffee.

It would be getting dark soon. Catherine stood at

the laced window and watched. Luke's car was not across the street and she wondered where he was. Like the seagulls, he was a bit of a mystery.

As she stood with the curtain parted just an inch, she saw a car with two men inside go slowly past; they seemed to be looking for someone or something. She'd seen them before. Knowing that Trini was being sought by two men, Catherine watched them until they disappeared from her line of vision. If only, she thought, there was a known reason for their search. Were they police officers or something more menacing?

She moved away from the window and sat down in the wooden rocking chair to think. At twenty-two, Trini was six years younger than Catherine. Her life had taken a turn in the wrong direction, taking the younger girl's actions to an existence of jeopardy. It was all so wrong. Catherine thought about what she'd been reluctantly told by her chief. Trini relied on drugs and, to obtain them, she had become a gopher for the dealers. She was young and pretty, and from all accounts, a bright girl with a talent for math. Everything could have and should have been positive for Trini, so why had this dangerous life persuaded her to comply?

Catherine fell asleep and woke to a darkened room and the sound of a car door closing. She moved quickly out of the rocker and toward the window. It was Luke. He was reaching into his pocket; standing at the door, he opened it to darkness and then light. Catherine watched as another light in the cottage illuminated what she assumed was his bathroom. She drew away from

15

the window, switching a dim light on in the main room. It was another quiet evening to endure. The street along the beach did not seem particularly safe, yet with hundreds of people, what could happen? She decided that she'd wait until nine or ten then she'd go out and have a look around. If this was Trini's hideaway, she'd have to show up at some point. Catherine wasn't sure what she'd say to her sister, but she was certain she'd think of something. As to leaving there, Catherine would not accept no for an answer. Things were going to change.

Catherine took a shower and changed into jeans and a navy blue jersey. She brushed her shoulder-length auburn hair and applied a skim of pale pink to her lips. With her purse on her right shoulder, she locked the door and left, observing that Luke's car was once again gone. She walked toward the cafés, alive with country music and the rancid smell of heavily buttered popcorn and beer. Laughter seemed to ring out from every corner and Catherine wondered what could possibly be so funny. She had never felt in tune with people who found humor in differences; quite often, she thought, people laughed at what should have been mended, or at crude remarks which should not have been spoken. She didn't get it and it somewhat set her apart.

At a small intersection, a crowd had gathered. Catherine inched closer and, as she did, she could see that a half-naked guitarist was performing in the middle of the street. He looked unsteady on his feet, but people were clapping in time to his rhythm and laughing at the scantily clad man who was obviously inebriated. Catherine smiled and shook her head, then moved on. It was, she supposed, a place where people who had jobs they hated or family discrepancies could gather to lose themselves for a while. Maybe everyone was just like the seagulls, in need of a place to hunker down.

Catherine walked past a t-shirt store and then turned around. In the photo of Trini, she was wearing a pink t-shirt. Catherine walked into the store, which reeked of marijuana. As a police officer, she was acquainted with the sweet aroma and, from what she'd learned, thought that her sister would be as well.

Catherine walked over to a clerk behind the counter, a man who looked to be about sixty and perfectly normal. When he asked if he could help her, Catherine produced the photo of Trini and asked if he'd seen her.

The man adjusted his eyeglasses and looked closely at the young woman's face.

"Pretty little thing," he said, "I think I've seen her, but during the course of a summer, I see thousands of people on this strip. I sure haven't seen her lately."

"This summer?" Catherine asked.

The man looked at the photo again and shook his head. "I don't think so, I'm not sure. Ask at Petra's, the hat and sunglass shop two doors down. Petra knows everyone."

Catherine thanked him and left. At Petra's, Catherine hesitated and then walked inside the tiny shop, again to the heavy aroma of marijuana. She looked around for a woman but saw only a young man. She went to him and asked if Petra was there. She was not. Catherine pulled the photo from her purse and showed the young man.

17

"Have you seen this girl?" she asked.

The young clerk looked at the picture, his eyes saying yes while his lips said no.

"Are you sure?" Catherine persisted.

"I'm sure," he said turning away. "I've never seen her before."

Catherine didn't believe him, but she had no authority to press him further.

After walking slowly throughout the beachside town for two more hours, Catherine bought herself another large coffee, hot this time, and made her way back to the cottage. It had been disappointing; there had been no sign of Trini anywhere.

Chapter Two

The evening spent within the walls of the small cottage was confining. Catherine sat down in the wooden rocker and watched as the cobalt sky turned to a blue-black. She wondered what to do next. Had this been a wise decision? She knew that her former chief had probably made sense when he told her to 'let it go' regarding her sister - easy for him to say. With thoughts of Trini on her mind, where the young girl could be, why she was being hunted by two suspected criminals, Catherine couldn't go on with everyday life. She had considered asking a detective friend on the force to help her, but knew it wouldn't be fair to implicate him and put his position at risk.

When Catherine opened her eyes, she realized she'd spent the night upright in the rocking chair. Her shoulders felt stiff. The last fence she'd scaled when running after a teen that had snatched a purse, had left her with a measure of pain in her right rotator cuff, and the left shoulder and wrist had endured a sprain. She looked down at her slim body. Maybe becoming a police officer hadn't been such a hot idea – she'd elected to follow in her father's footsteps.

She stood, stretched carefully then moved to the kitchen where she placed the kettle on the stove for tea. She walked to the bathroom and after giving her long hair a brushing before a small mirror, she walked back into the kitchen. It was both troubling and boring to be here alone, and as the kettle whistled, Catherine remembered her eleven o'clock date on the rocks with Luke Renoir.

After showering, changing into a pair of jeans and a dark blue blouse, which covered her slender hips, Catherine drank her tea and walked to the window. Luke's car was gone and she wondered if he had remembered their proposed meeting.

Just before eleven, she drove to the posh length of shoreline and the rocks where she had first encountered her new acquaintance. His car was not there. She sat for a few moments, then shut off her car's engine and slipped out into the fresh air. She looked around and saw a young family with their two children flying colorful kites on the grassy knoll behind her. Catherine walked toward the sea and sat almost exactly where she had been the previous day.

With sunglasses in place against the day's glare, Catherine looked out to the energized ocean and watched as gulls dipped and gracefully flew in tango rhythm as they circled the rocks in search of food. She thought of Luke's question – where do they rest at night? *Where? And where did Trini rest?*

"Good morning," he said. Catherine turned to see him carrying a brown bag in one hand, two cups of coffee balanced in the other.

Catherine scrambled to her feet to help with the coffee. "This smells good," she said.

Luke sat down close to where Catherine had perched earlier and with a slight hesitation, she sat down again in the same space, one foot of glimmering granite separating them.

"I have cranberry-walnut scones," he said with a smile as he placed his paper cup on a flat rock and opened the bag. He held it toward Catherine and she reached in for a treat.

"Were you waiting long?" he asked.

"No," she said swallowing a small, delicious bite, "a few minutes. These are wonderful, where did you get them?"

"On the edge of town; there's a bakery there I like."

They sat quietly, each observing the rolling sea as they drank coffee and ate their scones. Catherine wanted to ask him questions about why he was there, about who was in his life, about the black clothing she'd first seen him wearing. She said nothing.

"So, you're Catherine," he said as he tossed crumbs toward the hopeful gulls.

She looked at him and wondered what he'd meant to imply. Was he saying that he knew of her, that he'd heard about her search, or was he just reaffirming whom she had introduced herself as? "Yes," she said, "that's right."

He smiled as she tossed tiny pieces of scone toward the waiting gulls. They were quiet for a few moments when Catherine took the sunglasses from her blue eyes and looked into Luke's eyes of dark brown.

"Do you know Trini?" she asked with a forced bravado.

"Who?" he asked.

Catherine could tell by his expression that he had

21

no idea what she was talking about. She looked at him for a few seconds and then looked away.

"Who's Trini?" he asked.

Catherine looked back at him. She studied his handsome features for a few moments and then she looked away again.

"Is this person a friend?" he asked after taking a few swallows of coffee.

Catherine shook her head from side to side. "No," she said.

Luke was quiet as he observed Catherine's refined profile, the long, curved lashes at her piercing blue eyes. As he studied her beautiful face, she suddenly turned and looked at him, her long auburn hair sweeping across her lips. She pulled the strands away from her nose and mouth and then met his stare. "Who are you?" she asked.

He smiled. "I told you my name, but you're wondering about more than that, aren't you?"

Catherine didn't answer as she kept her eyes on his.

Luke sighed, finished his coffee, then crushed the cup and put it into the brown bag. He tucked it beneath his right thigh so that it wouldn't blow away. His eyes followed the gulls as they circled above them then he looked directly into Catherine's eyes.

"Where do I begin?" he asked as he turned and stared at his black shoes.

"Maybe with the truth?" she suggested.

Luke looked at her, at the sea, then back at Catherine. "I told you I was a fraud. I am. I was a priest. I am no longer with the church, but occasionally,

I pretend to be."

Catherine squinted against the sun. "Why would you do such a thing?"

Luke moved his legs so that his knees pointed to the sky. He looped his arms around his legs and stared straight ahead.

"I suppose so that I wouldn't disappoint my aunt, my Godmother. She'd be crushed if she knew I'd left the priesthood."

Catherine felt she needed much more in the way of an explanation, but she waited.

"I was a priest for a few years when I realized I'd made this life-altering decision for all the wrong reasons. I left. I haven't been a priest for about a year and a half."

Catherine sat numbed trying to digest what he had said.

"What about you?" he asked. "The cottage, the strip of beach near town, they're not your style. What are you hiding from?"

"I don't understand," she said avoiding his question. "Why are you staying in the cottage across from me? What does leaving the priesthood have to do with you being here?"

Luke moved his feet just a bit and looked away from her. "My mother died in my arms when I was fourteen. She had an aneurism. It left me and my little sister, who was nine at the time, with a grieving father. My Godmother stepped in, helped us to cope. She's my mother's older sister. She urged me to college and then the seminary. I felt lost, like I'd never dare to have a relationship for fear of losing it as my father had; it all just fell into place. I became a priest. I knew almost immediately that I'd made a mistake. I wasn't up to the task and I didn't want that incredibly lonely life. I wasn't good at a pretty important job."

Catherine thought about what he said and then asked, "So, why the beach cottage? What are you doing with your life now?"

Luke looked at Catherine as he spoke. "I came here to stay for a few weeks because my Godmother, who has no idea I've left the priesthood, is summering nearby. She expected to see me because I was once assigned to a private school a few miles away. She's leaving for North Carolina soon; when I see her in the future, it will be to visit her there. She's having some health issues and will live with my cousin. I feel like I'm deceiving her, but I think it would break her heart if she knew I was teaching in a private, non-Catholic college. Some things are better kept secret."

Catherine looked from Luke to the ocean. She wasn't so sure he was right.

"What about you?" he asked. "What brings you here?"

Catherine took a deep breath. "I'm looking for my half-sister."

"Is this the Trini you mentioned?"

Catherine nodded. They were quiet for a few moments.

"Is it anything you want to talk about?"

"Not really," she said.

Luke looked away and then stood, gathering the brown paper bag in his hands.

"I should go," he said. "I'm having an early dinner

with Ruthie."

Catherine gave him a questioning look.

"Ruthie is my aunt and Godmother. But I'd like to connect with you again if you have time. Are you busy later this evening?"

Catherine looked up at his tall form and shielded her eyes from the sun with one hand. "What time?"

"I'll be back by eight, any time after that would work for me."

Catherine stood and started to walk back toward her car, Luke at her side.

"Where would we go?" she asked.

"I'd invite you to my place," he said with a smile, "but I'm sure it's similar if not the same as yours, not great for entertaining. Are you familiar with Ricardo's?"

"I think I've passed it. It's the restaurant further down from here, right?"

"Right," Luke said. "We could have a drink, a bite to eat if you wish; it's a relaxing place with some nice outdoor seating."

Catherine kept pace with his long, lanky strides. "It might be a nice change," she said.

Luke laughed. "Well, thanks. I think we could both use a change of scenery. And maybe you'll tell me *your* story."

Catherine ran her hand through her windblown hair. "Why do you think I have a story?"

"Trini?" he reminded her.

Catherine looked down at the steps she was taking and was relieved when they reached their cars.

"Do you want to meet me at Ricardo's or would

you like to ride with me? I could swing by and pick you up around eight-thirty."

"I'll meet you there," she said, and they parted.

It was after two when Catherine walked into her cottage, placed her shoulder purse on a chair and walked to the kitchen. She had enjoyed the scone, but that was a few hours ago and she was hungry. She ate an orange and then made tea, thinking about what she would wear on her excursion to Ricardo's later in the evening. The only outfit she had with her that was even close to being appropriate for a nice restaurant was a brilliant red, sleeveless blouse and a knee-length skirt in off white. She decided that with white sandals, she'd be okay.

Feeling tired and frustrated, Catherine went to the bed in her room and as she began to doze, she heard a door slam at the cottage next to hers; a voice said something guttural and unrecognizable, but there was a profound statement in the way the words had been delivered in anger. She sat up on her bed then peered outside to see the form of a young man slip into a black car. He started the engine, backed out of the shallow driveway, and sped away. Catherine stood and looked at the pale green cottage just ten or twelve feet from her own. The quality of people staying in this community was not high. She hated that her sister was accustomed to this mode of living amidst drinking, drugs and danger.

Catherine looked at the darkened windows of the green cottage and wondered who had been left behind, a battered wife or girlfriend? A drug deal gone bad? This, she thought, was a perplexing place. It was a honky-tonk beach strip with about one-hundred tiny cottages crunched together just a few miles away from thriving mansions, gorgeous beaches, clubs and restaurants.

She turned away and thought about Luke. He had given up on a vocation, a life of solitary commitment to his God, a life removed from the intricacies of relationships and duties to a family of his own. He was interesting. And there she was, donning a uniform and going out into a world of crime prevention and detection, yet afraid of everything. No solid relationships for Catherine – too risky, dead end.

She slid back onto the bed and closed her eyes. She would rest for a while before she'd walk the strip. Trini could appear at any time. Or, she could not. Catherine had no idea where to look for the girl other than here in this bedlam. How could they be related and yet be so different?

At the busiest part of the day, Catherine walked to the assortment of cafés and shops where you could buy anything from food to feathered boas in bright neon colors. One young girl passed her in the street – she was laughing with her arms around a bare-chested male wearing a bright pink boa and a white cowboy hat. Catherine smiled, they were young and crazy, but they were having obvious fun.

With her eyes scanning the scantily-clad bodies and the shops filled with mostly souvenirs and unnecessary items, Catherine walked. She bought herself an iced coffee, sipping it through a thick straw as she moved. At one point, she saw a girl with blonde braids – two, but when she saw her face, Catherine

27

realized it wasn't Trini.

By six o'clock, she had turned around and was heading back toward the cottage. She would spruce herself up, change her clothes, and then she'd drive to Ricardo's to meet Luke. That relationship was like a beast with two heads – he was handsome and a little mysterious, and he was intriguing. She wished she hadn't found him appealing, she wished she hadn't found him at all. He was distracting.

At eight-twenty-five Catherine pulled into the well-groomed parking area of Ricardo's and saw Luke leaning against his car. He was wearing tan slacks and a black shirt. She parked next to him and when she stepped out of her car, his eyes moved over her body and not in a reverent way.

"That's a pretty shirt," he said as he took in the red fabric and then her blue eyes.

"That's a nice shirt you have on as well," she said, "very priestly in color."

Luke smiled. "It's a hard habit to break and, besides, I like black. Ready?" he asked as they began to walk toward the restaurant's patio with a view of the sea.

Catherine walked beside him holding her long hair back, secured from the cool evening breeze. He watched her, and as they sat down, he helped position her chair.

They ordered a tray of appetizers and two glasses of wine. Catherine wondered what they were doing here, why she'd agreed to this unexpected evening.

Luke caught her looking at him and he smiled. "Something on your mind?" he asked.

Catherine moved her eyes to the others around them and then to the ocean, the waves rhythmically lapping at the rocks nearby.

"Just curiosity," she said. "I never knew anyone who'd left the priesthood."

"Did you ever know a priest?"

Catherine nodded. "Sure, they sat next to me at Sunday dinner quite often. I grew up Catholic and my parents were good friends with two different priests from our parish."

"Ah," Luke said. "So you're Catholic."

"Not really," Catherine said. "I was brought up in the church, but I drifted away. I have no specific idea why, I just did."

Their wine arrived and they each took a few sips.

"I'm glad we could do this tonight," he said.

Catherine looked at him, the wine glass suspended in mid-air. "Why?"

Luke laughed. "You do ask some pointed questions. I guess the answer would be because it's been boring and lonely. I'm not exactly crazy about the cottage, but it's pricey to stay elsewhere. I needed to hang around for my aunt's duration in the area, but I was forced to settle for what I could find that was available and affordable. Now, what's your story?"

"I told you, my sister."

"You didn't tell me much."

Catherine looked away and then back into his soft, dark eyes. "It's hard to explain."

"Try," he urged. "I'm a good listener."

Catherine laughed. "I'll bet you are. Hear any good confessions?"

29

Luke smiled. "Yes, and I heard a few bad ones, too."

"I hated going to confession," Catherine said.

"Me too," he replied.

They were silent until the appetizers arrived. Luke used a colorful toothpick to move a hot pepper into his mouth. He made a face then claimed it was good.

They ate, had a second glass of wine, then walked along a length of smooth beach.

During a period of silence except for the gentle splash of waves on the shore, Catherine said, "She's my half-sister."

Luke looked at her as they walked. She was beautiful.

"When I was five, my parents broke up. My mother and I went to stay with my grandparents. Dad had an affair. A year or so later, Mom and Dad got back together, but in the break-up time, Trini was born to Dad and a woman from Germany."

Luke raised his eyebrows. "That must have gone over well with your mother."

"She didn't know about it until Dad was dying. He was a policeman, retired, getting ready to spend his days fly-fishing. He was diagnosed with cancer and, within a year, he was gone. On his deathbed, he told Mom about Trini."

"Wow. When was that?"

"Ten months ago."

Luke walked quietly alongside Catherine.

"After Dad died, Mom moved to Arizona to be near her sister. And I suspect to get away from everything she'd had to endure – Dad's death, the news about Trini."

"Does she know you're looking for Trini?" And then, as if it occurred to Luke that Catherine might not know her own sister, he stopped walking and looked at Catherine. She stopped and looked back.

"Have *you* met Trini?"

Catherine started to walk slowly. "No."

They were speechless again for a few minutes and during that time, Catherine's suspicious nature began to focus on disturbing questions. What if Luke had never been a priest at all? What if he was somehow involved with Trini's disappearance? Catherine swallowed and thought how stupidly naïve she had been. This handsome man at her side might be exactly what he'd claimed when they first met, a fraud.

At a cluster of large rock formations where the sea was flirting with stone, Luke stopped, stuffed his hands in his trouser pockets and looked at Catherine.

"I'm sure you're not going to be surprised when I say that I don't understand. I thought you were searching for your sister, a sister you knew."

Catherine chose her words carefully. "I found out about having a half-sister after my father was gone. I was angry. I would have liked knowing about her, maybe being close to her somehow, but it was all a deep, dark secret. All I know is that Trini's mother was here from Germany, working as a nanny. My father had a relationship with her for about two months, which resulted in Trini. My sister was born in Germany, but came here as a nanny herself a few years ago."

"That's all you know?"

Catherine looked into Luke's beautiful eyes and

31

wished she didn't feel bonded to him. "When I decided to look for her, I found that she'd left her nanny position and was drifting in this area with unsavory companions. The word is that she's been into the drug scene. I need to find her."

"And you think she's here?"

"A drug cohort of hers was picked up for questioning and said that the beach strip has been her chosen hangout. I have no other leads."

"How did you learn all this?" he asked.

Carefully, not at all certain that she should explain, Catherine swallowed and said, "From the police in our town where the fellow was brought in. He was known to hang out with Trini and a few others. I tried to learn more, but I was closed out of the information and told I'd be kept informed."

Catherine purposely neglected to tell Luke that two men were searching for Trini. What if one of them was Luke?

Walking along the hardened sand of the beach back toward Ricardo's, Catherine's bare arm brushed against Luke's and she felt a chill. She believed that something was intrinsically wrong with her emotions, that she could ambiguously feel attraction for him as well as suspicion.

At their cars, Catherine pressed her key to unlock the car's door and Luke opened it, standing so that she could not slip inside. "Do you," he said, "consider that you could be putting yourself in danger? If these people your sister has been keeping company with are serious drug pushers, you could present a problem to them. They could think you're after them and not just your sister."

Catherine squirmed and hoped she'd hidden her reaction well. "I know," she said.

Luke moved aside so that Catherine could move in behind her steering wheel.

"I have a question," he said as he started to close the door and watched Catherine fasten her seat belt. "If it's none of my business, that's fine, but I'm curious. What kind of work do you do?"

Catherine looked in her rear-view mirror and then at Luke. "Nothing at the moment, but I was a police officer."

Luke's face showed his surprise. "You're kidding," he said.

"Not at all. Why, because I'm a woman?"

Luke smiled. "A *beautiful* woman."

Catherine felt her lips begin to stretch into a reciprocating smile as she forced herself to maintain a serious expression. "Your willingness to share a compliment is interesting," she said.

Luke laughed. "Well, when you're a priest, you're sort of off limits. I guess some people would think we weren't threatening. It's sometimes amusing to be able to be a non-person, someone who isn't being complimentary to gain personally."

"Incognito man," she murmured.

"Sort of, except that sometimes it doesn't work."

Catherine looked up at him. He was way too handsome as he leaned against her car, his face just inches from hers. "And what is that supposed to mean?" she asked.

Luke straightened up and tucked his hands back

into his pockets. "We'll save that story for another time," he said.

Another time? Catherine started her engine. "This was nice," she said. "I'm sure I'll see you around."

"Eleven for coffee on the rocks tomorrow?"

Catherine smiled. "Sure. I'll bring the coffee this time. How do you take yours?"

"Black."

She rolled up her window and backed out of her space. Driving off, she looked through the rear-view mirror. Catherine could see him standing there next to his car; she had all she could do to resist turning around to plant a firm kiss on his luxuriously full lips.

"I'm way too bored with this business of living alone in a miserable little cottage," she said to herself. With her window cracked for a breath of salt air, ten minutes later she was back in her own driveway.

Chapter Three

When Catherine woke up the next day, she was surprised that she'd slept three hours longer than usual. She'd walked the beach strip the night before, mentally and physically spent. There had been multiple maybes within the throngs of people in the streets, young blondes, blending with pairs of shapely legs and minimally covered torsos. Catherine watched too, for the young men who walked in sets of two. She examined each face for signs of stress, anger, violent ambitions. All she noted were drinks in hand and laughing voices. There were no indications of ill-doing or of anything particularly illegal. It was, in fact, an open display of how to live carelessly without thought of modesty or inhibition.

She thought about going out for coffee then remembered that she was bringing coffee for herself and Luke at eleven. She slipped into the shower and then into jeans and a loose fitting lavender-colored blouse. She combed her long hair and thought about Luke having been a priest. She'd never known a priest who'd left his religious life behind. Had it to do with church policies regarding recent items in the news? What gave him cause to change his mind about a powerful life decision? And then, was the story true or a cover-up? What exactly made Luke Renoir the fraud

35

he'd admitted to being?

Choosing her steps carefully as she moved along the smooth rock formations, Catherine glanced up momentarily to see Luke sitting with his back to her, as he intently focused his dark eyes on the brilliant sea. She stopped for a moment and sat down just a foot away from him. He looked at her and smiled, no words necessary.

Catherine handed him a container of coffee and a small white bag.

"What's the prize?" he asked as he looked inside.

"Pumpkin spice doughnuts," she said. "I thought that since they're made with pumpkin, we could claim to be eating vegetables."

"Works for me," he said with a smile as he reached into the bag.

They were quiet for a few minutes as they each sipped coffee and ate their late-morning breakfast, sharing crumbs with the gulls.

"I've been thinking about you," Luke said. "I still can't get my mind wrapped around you being a policewoman."

"Police *officer*," she corrected with a slight smile.

Luke nodded. "Sorry. I'm learning to be politically correct. But really, you just don't seem the type."

"What's the type?" Catherine asked. "I really liked it."

"Are you through with it?" Luke asked.

Why, she wondered, would he ask that?

"Yes. Like everything else, it's a lot about who you know, who you decide to agree or disagree with. I'm okay with moving on."

"And," he said, "what's next?"

Catherine took a swallow of coffee and looked out to the incoming tide. "For now, I'm spending my efforts looking for my sister. Later, I think I'll go back to school. I have a degree in the social sciences, but I'm pretty fond of books. I might try for a degree in library science, or maybe I'll just open a little book shop someplace."

Luke nodded and they were quiet.

"Where are you teaching now?" Catherine asked as she glanced at her attractive companion.

"Vermont," he replied.

Catherine smiled and said, "Well, you're a long way from home here in Rhode Island."

Luke continued to stare at the sea, watching the gulls dip for the occasional crab or clamshell on the patch of sand that was still dry. "That's true," he said, "but since this is where Ruthie expects me to be, I'm tied here, and not unwillingly. This is a pretty nice stretch of earth."

Catherine looked out to the crashing waves. "Do you miss this in Vermont?"

Luke shook his head. "No, not so much. I'm a few hours away – when I need an ocean fix, I can get to beaches all up and down the coast. And I like the mountains, they're peaceful."

"So, you'll go back there in a few weeks?"

Luke nodded. "It's a small college; they start up again the third week of September."

Another month or so, Catherine calculated, and then he'd be gone. Why did that thought trouble her? She had no idea what it was about him that drew her in.

His looks were outstanding, but she'd known other attractive men. His mannerisms were gentle and his words often philosophical, but more than that, he'd managed to set her heart into a faster pace – that hadn't been the case for more than six years and never to this extent.

"What are you doing with the rest of your day?" he asked.

Catherine shrugged her slim shoulders. "More of the same. I'll walk downtown and keep my eyes out for Trini."

"Does she look like you?" Luke asked as he glanced at her pretty profile, the long hair strands drifting over her lips and neck.

"No, I'm sure she must resemble her mother. Trini's hair is as blonde as mine is dark."

Luke stood and moved behind her, squatting down, his hands gently gathering her long hair together.

"What are you doing?" Catherine asked with a pang of fear in her thoughts.

"After my mother died, someone needed to fix my little sister's hair each morning. The only thing I was good at was braiding, and I'm still pretty good at it."

Catherine could feel his deft fingers brushing against her neck as he maneuvered her long tresses into a single braid. Odd that he would do this, not only to a virtual stranger, but to Trini's sister – Trini who was known always to wear her hair in this style.

After several minutes of feeling the slight tugs and gentle twisting, Luke moved back to his seat on the rocks.

"How did you do that?" she asked. "What did you

38

use to fasten the ends?"

Luke laughed. "Your own hair. I was used to having a ready elastic band or ribbon for my sister, but when I didn't, I found a way to use the hair itself. Don't worry, it comes undone easily."

Catherine reached back and felt her hair firmly fastened; she thanked him as he appraised her beautiful face.

Slightly shaken from his touch, his long fingers to her bare skin, Catherine purposely looked away from him for a few moments. Was her interest in him apparent? She was astounded with herself for admitting to a weakness in the knees when it came to Luke Renoir – she hoped it wasn't obvious.

"Do you want to do something later?" he asked.

Catherine squinted against the bright sun reflecting on the water. "Like what?"

"I don't know," Luke said. "We could do a repeat of last night at Ricardo's, or we could see a movie. Or maybe you'd like company roaming the beach strip. It might not make you look so vulnerable if you were taking a leisurely stroll like the rest of the crowd."

"Have you done that, strolled with the crowd in town?"

Luke nodded. "Yup, did that to case the area when I first arrived here in early July."

Catherine laughed. "I hope you weren't disguised as a priest."

Luke smiled. "I tried to blend in whenever I wasn't meeting with Ruthie."

Catherine squirmed and readjusted her position on the hard surface. "I'm curious," she said. "Have you ever been, you know, involved?"

Luke tilted his head back and laughed. "My, aren't you discreet. Are you asking if I've been with a woman?"

Catherine pursed her lips then smiled. "I guess so."

Luke took a moment to allow his eyes to examine her face. "A long time ago."

Catherine's expression changed to a serious look. "Really?"

Luke scuffed at the rock with one foot then stretched his long legs out before him, as if he had nothing to hide.

"Yeah. I was trying to find my way. I was in college, eighteen years old."

"And?"

Luke laughed again. "You're unrelenting. And, she and I found a pastime we both enjoyed for a while. She was looking for entertainment, I was looking for nothing."

Catherine shook her head. "You guys are all alike, aren't you?"

"Do you mean priests, or males in general?"

"I'm thinking that most men are pretty much the same."

Luke shook his head from side to side. "Not true. I was young. I was slightly stupid. Sex was everywhere. I'm looking forward to something a little more meaningful in the future."

Catherine stared at him. "You told me you'd left the priesthood a year and a half ago. Are you saying you've been alone?"

Once again, Luke smiled. "Catherine, I love the

way you tip-toe around your questions. 'Alone', now that's an interesting way to ask if I've been sexually active since leaving the priesthood. To answer, yes, I have been 'alone'."

Catherine felt her face grow warm and was certain that the blush was obvious. She decided to say nothing in return, but it crossed her mind that she wouldn't mind giving him a few lessons.

"So," he began, "now that you've extracted personal information out of me, you owe me this evening. Where are we going?"

Catherine smiled at him, her blue eyes twinkling with mischief and warmth. "I could treat you to a burger on the strip, and then we could meander around. I'll show you the picture of Trini, then we can both watch for her."

"I'm in," he said with a flirty look into her eyes and then to her slightly parted lips.

When they left the rocky shore, they walked in unison until they reached their cars. Catherine did not waste time getting in behind the wheel. Luke seemed hesitant, but then he waved and told her he'd see her around six back at the cottages.

Catherine drove to her driveway and, as she approached, she saw a young man with light hair leaving the cottage next to hers. He was wearing a bright green t-shirt and gray slacks; he seemed uninterested in greeting her or anyone else. She wondered if it had been him she'd heard speaking in angry tones, and she wondered who was inside putting up with his verbal abuse.

After he drove away, Catherine went inside her

41

own cottage and stood near to her bedroom window, close enough to see the green cottage, but not be seen. She stared at the window, darkened by daylight shadows, and imagined who might be there, looking back. With a sense of doubt and caution, Catherine decided she needed to borrow a screwdriver and walked next door where she knocked gently. She listened and heard nothing. She knocked harder, still there was nothing. Maybe the place is empty, she thought. After all, she'd been with Luke for the past few hours; anyone could have left that cottage while she was gone.

Catherine walked back to her own place and made tea. She wandered from window to window, watching, always looking for the face in her photograph, or for men who seemed suspiciously looking around. Her fervent hope was that the two men said to be searching for Trini had not found her.

Catherine took her purse and decided to walk downtown for a coffee; the tea was not what she wanted at this point, and she would buy more oranges as well. With the photo of her sister tucked into her purse, she walked into a small café, sat down at the counter and ordered. On a whim, she extracted the picture from its darkened space and showed it to the waitress. "Have you seen this girl?"

The woman placed the glass coffee pot back on its stand and took the photo of Trini in her hands. "Yeah," she said, "she used to come in here all the time. Haven't seen her in a while though. Why? Did she do something wrong? She's a nice kid, not the type to get into stuff, you know what I mean?"

"Yes," Catherine said. "She's a friend; I had hoped

to see her along the beach area."

"Well," the woman shook her head, "you could. She's a pretty little thing, not really what we see around here in summer."

"Thank you," Catherine said for both coffee and information. Trini had been there – she was recognizable, distinctive in her wholesome, milkmaid looks. It was beginning to feel more than frightening; it was discouraging to know that Trini might be there, but in hiding. How would Catherine find her sister if she was being elusive? There seemed to be few options except for keeping eyes and ears open to any possibilities. The girl had not attempted to return to Germany – she was somewhere nearby and that's all Catherine knew for sure.

When six o'clock came, Catherine saw Luke start to walk toward her cottage and she met him outside. She had left her jeans on and replaced the lavender shirt with one of black. She also left her hair in Luke's braid. He looked at her and smiled as they met in the middle of the narrow street.

"Aren't you looking priestly," he teased.

"And you aren't," she said, taking note of his chino pants and white shirt with its sleeves rolled back.

"Where are we heading?" he asked as they walked toward town.

"There's a little burger place called Turk's. Have you been there? The burgers aren't as greasy as most along the strip."

Luke laughed. "Great recommendation; let's go, I love burgers and I'm starved."

"Wait," she said, "I want to show you a picture of

43

Trini. Please, if you see a blonde, even if not a braided blonde, tell me. I'm desperate to find her."

Luke took a long look at the picture, his face somber. "Okay," he said as he returned the photo and they walked on, each of them scanning the faces of more under thirties people than they had ever seen before.

Catherine found that walking with Luke gave her a sense of relief, not to be alone in the search, not to seem different from the others teamed up or grouped together. After eating and strolling the area until after ten, Luke invited Catherine for a drink.

"I try to stay alert," she said. "I'm not much of a drinker anyway, but especially now, I feel like I'm always on guard looking for Trini. It's exhausting."

Luke looked at her, his eyes traveling the thick auburn braid. "You look nothing alike," he said. "You and your sister are as different as night and day."

"I know," she said.

"A drink doesn't have to be alcohol," Luke reasoned. "We could have a raspberry lime-rickey, or a lemonade crush."

Catherine smiled as they neared a stand selling cold drinks. "I'd love a raspberry lime-rickey," she said.

Luke ordered two and then they walked on toward their cottages.

Standing before Catherine's cottage, Luke finished his drink and looked down at her. "Tired?" he asked.

Catherine knew that question, that tone. He meant that he'd like to continue the evening, at her place or his. Like him as she did, she wasn't ready for that, and she *was* tired.

"Yes," she said, "I'm worn down. But I enjoyed tonight – it was really a wonderful change to have company. Thank you, Luke."

He looked at her with his hands tucked into his trouser pockets, almost as if he was afraid what he might do with those hands if they were free.

"I'll let you go then," he said. "Coffee at eleven on the rocks?"

Catherine nodded. "Okay."

"I'll get it and see you there," he said, then he turned and crossed the street. Inside, Catherine ran her right forefinger over her lips and wondered. She left her purse in a chair and walked to the wooden rocker. She fell asleep and woke at three in the morning when she heard a car door slam at the green cottage next door. At first, she was stunned with the loud sound echoing in her ears then she stood and walked to the bedroom window. It was dark in her room and it looked dark next door. She saw the red taillights of the car pulling away. It troubled her; something was not right in that house. She had only seen a man entering and leaving, and yet he'd been cussing and angry with whoever was left behind. Every possible negative brought Catherine thoughts of Trini. The man she saw did not seem to fit the typical person involved with drugs, and that's who she believed was looking for Trini. This man was clean cut, someone not expected to dwell in this community, which made Catherine think that perhaps he was bickering with and possibly abusing his wife or girlfriend. The police officer in her made her want to intervene, but she had her limits. She was already in hot water with her former chief over her persistence about her sister's disappearance. She was nowhere with this investigation. Catherine had so hoped to find Trini, to give her a chance at good health and perhaps even transportation out of harm's way, back to Germany if necessary. Catherine was not giving up. She moved out of her bedroom and went to the kitchen where she made tea and stared outside until the sky was light.

In the small bathroom sink, she washed a few undergarments and two blouses. She hung them on hangers to dry and then looked at what she might wear for her meeting with Luke. He brightened her life with his presence. Although she knew that when he left it would be impossibly boring to wait within the cottage for some sign of Trini or the men in pursuit of her, she had no options. Catherine stepped out of her jeans, into pale pink shorts and a white jersey. She took her hair from the braid and liked the way the style left her hair with a wavy look.

In the kitchen, Catherine drank tea and ate an orange. She missed her apartment with its nice oven and microwave. This place was meant to be a shelter and not much more. She thought about what she would do when her time here was through. She would give herself another month here at least, then after that, she would need to think about her future. She had some savings, some of it a gift from her father's will, but it wouldn't last forever.

Catherine slipped her feet into her sandals and stepped outside for a breath of fresh air. It was humid, not usual for the beach area, but, still, the air was heavy with the threat of rain. What would that do to her date with Luke? By nine-thirty, it was raining and Catherine looked across the street to Luke's driveway. The car was gone. She stood at the window and watched, but no one was out in the wet weather and with rain against windows, it was hard to define passengers going by in cars.

Catherine sat down in the rocker, she would drive to the rocky shores just before eleven – maybe she and Luke could share coffee in his or her car.

Thinking it could be chilly, she took a dark pink cardigan with her when she left and drove to the shoreline, dotted with mansions across the street from the sleepless tides. Two miles away from the beach town's center, the difference was incredible. Unfair, was the word that came to Catherine's mind; unjustly distributed wealth – some with everything, others with nothing.

At their chosen section of rocky shore, Catherine pulled into a space. She was there alone, no one else brave enough to face the rain and wind. She looked down at her bare legs and thought she'd made a poor choice – should have worn jeans. And then she wondered if Luke would show up.

Just before eleven, his car pulled into the space next to hers. He got out, opened her passenger door and slipped in.

"Hi," he said. "I see you're all set for a nice swim." His eyes went to her bare legs.

"My wardrobe here is limited. I suppose this is a weird outfit for a rainy day."

"On the contrary, you're a ray of sunshine on this raw, damp day. As you can see, I have no coffee. I

47

thought we could go to Ricardo's and have brunch. What do you think?"

Before Catherine could answer, he opened the door and said, "Come on, hop in my car and we'll go. It'll be my treat."

Catherine took her keys, purse and sweater and moved quickly to Luke's car. "This is kind of fun," she said as she slipped the seat belt over her shoulder and watched Luke's hands at the wheel and gearshift. His hands were beautiful. He could have been a piano player with those long, slim fingers, the square shape of his hand, the trimmed nails. Everything about this man was almost too good to be true.

They drove in silence, every now and then one glanced at the other, like two kids on their first date. When they pulled into Ricardo's, Luke told Catherine to stay put; he had an umbrella they could share. At her car door, he opened it and took her hand to pull her closer to him as they huddled beneath the black umbrella and moved quickly toward the restaurant's door. Inside, they were seated at a table where the view was always spectacular. Coffee was served as they browsed the menu.

At one point, Catherine looked up from reading and found Luke watching her. She was taken aback, but when he smiled, she smiled. It was sweet and it was awkward. She wanted to reach out for his hand. She resisted.

They each ordered an omelet with vegetables. When he noticed that the candle on their table was not lit, Luke lit it using a match from a tiny canister next to a bouquet of white daisies.

Catherine watched him. She remembered how direct and precise the priests had been, pouring just enough wine into the chalice, placing linen cloths down on the altar, smoothing them. Luke had those movements – he was delicate and delectable to observe. Catherine nearly smiled as she thought about the fact that she had never before thought of a priest as delectable, but no one had ever affected her the way that Luke Renoir had. Was this what people meant by unconditional whatever? She could not label her feelings as love; what was it? It was unconditional something and it made her a little more than careful in what she said and how she reacted to him. It was unnerving.

When a fresh carafe of coffee arrived, Luke took charge and poured the steaming black brew into their white porcelain cups. They each took sips, careful not to burn their mouths with the hot liquid.

"This is so good," Catherine said.

Luke agreed. "This is better than coffee on the rocks in the rain," he said with a smile. "There's nothing like a rainy day to demand focus. It's a good time to put order in our lives – no outside temptations."

"I suppose so," Catherine said. "I remember days like this when I was a kid. My mom made me clean out closets, tidy bureau drawers. Having brunch by the sea is much nicer."

"Do you have siblings other than Trini?" he asked.

"No. My parents were married several years before I was born. They were told their chances of conceiving were limited."

Luke smiled. "Sounds like you were a surprise."

Catherine sipped her coffee then replied, "I think so. And you have a sister."

"Right, Annie. She's married and lives in Kentucky. Her husband boards horses and Annie teaches first grade. They have two kids, James who is five and Ella who just turned two."

"You told me that your mother died, how is your father?"

Luke looked out to the sea for a moment then back at Catherine. "He was devastated after my mother died. He's lived in Florida for the past several years with my aunt and uncle, Dad's brother and his wife. He's okay; he's just not what I'd call a happy man."

Catherine nodded and, at that moment, their food was delivered. After enjoying their brunch, Luke leaned back in his chair and looked at Catherine. "How old did you say you were when your parents separated?"

"Between five and six."

"That must have been hard."

"It was confusing. I wasn't old enough to extract myself from the situation; I remember it as feeling divided. It was really kind of awful."

Luke observed her sad expression and said nothing more of the incident.

"Today," he said, "is not a great day to wander the streets of the beach area. What are your plans? I'm meeting Ruthie for an early dinner, around four. Would you like to join us?"

Catherine laughed softly. "And how would you explain me, Father?"

Luke bit on his lower lip and understood that Catherine was teasing him. "It's not very nice of you to keep this going you know. If you'd like to come along to meet Ruthie, I could think of something."

"We could tell her I'm a nun," she continued to taunt.

Luke reached across the table and poked her hand with a fork. "Not nice," he reminded her.

Catherine laughed again. "I think I'll pass. You might be okay with concealing your present life, but I'm a terrible liar. I think I'll hang out at the cottage. I have a book I haven't even opened – it's a good day to read."

They were quiet for a few moments, each of them taking a glimpse of the other when least likely to be noticed.

"Catherine," Luke said, "is there anything I could do to help you find your sister? I have time. I'm willing."

Catherine's eyes clouded with tears. "I wouldn't know what to ask of you. I don't know what I'm doing myself, Luke. All I know is that Trini is missing. Two men are looking for her and we don't know why. We know it isn't for anything good – I'm sure they mean to harm her."

"Are you privy to any information from the police?" he asked.

"Not really. I have a friend on the force. He called me once after I came here to tell me about the two men. I hadn't known anything about them when I first arrived. He said he'd let me know if there was anything else."

They folded their napkins on the table, Luke paid the bill and they left to find that a soft drizzle had replaced the pouring rain. Luke offered the umbrella and Catherine said she'd be fine without it. He drove her to her car in silence. As she moved to leave for her own car, he asked, "Are you ever afraid?"

Catherine looked ahead at the sea and their rocks. "Only when I think of those men reaching Trini before I do."

That afternoon and evening, Catherine felt restless. She read for a while, then found herself walking in puddle-ridden streets breathing heavy, humid air. She stopped and bought herself a raspberry lime-rickey where she'd enjoyed one with Luke. She thought about him dutifully dining with his aunt and smiled. He was something.

There were less than half the usual pedestrians walking the beach strip, but Catherine was glad for the change. If Trini was there, it might be easier to find her in a smaller crowd. At one point, she saw a blonde with two braids and Catherine hurried to catch a glimpse of her. The girl was young, maybe sixteen, and Catherine wondered who was missing her. What was this kid doing in a place like this?

By nine-thirty, Catherine was tired and hungry. She bought a large pretzel from a vendor and walked back to the cottage where she planted herself in the wooden rocking chair for the rest of the evening.

Chapter Four

Catherine woke at two in the morning to the sound of sirens. She ran to the front window in time to see an ambulance and police car heading toward town. Her immediate thought was of Trini. She pulled on a denim jacket and with only her keys in her hand, she walked quickly toward town. She could see the red and blue lights flashing a distance ahead and the beat of her heart was heavy and fast. There was always that dire possibility that her sister was involved.

Where the emergency vehicles stopped, Catherine slowed her pace, understanding that she needed to stay out of the way. Through blurbs of one-sentence conversations, she discovered that there had been a fire, a meth lab had exploded. She hoped with all her heart it did not involve her sister. She watched as a young man was taken on a stretcher to the ambulance. A woman in her thirties or early forties and a man about the same age were taken in handcuffs to a cruiser. Catherine stood back and breathed a sigh of relief.

As she began to turn toward her cottage, her arm was grabbed and she was being pulled aside. Startled, Catherine looked up at the shadowed face and felt a strong sense of fright.

"Catherine," he said pulling her close, "what in God's name are you doing in this?"

It was only when he spoke that Catherine realized Luke was at her side, and then she wondered why.

"I heard the sirens," she said.

Luke loosened his grip on her. "Catherine, this could have been dangerous. These people often have weapons. You shouldn't have come down here."

Catherine took a deep breath and started to walk beside Luke.

"What were you doing here?" she asked accusingly.

"I heard the sirens, too. I saw you leave. As soon as I could pull on some jeans and a shirt, I came running." He ran his hand through his thick hair. "You're kind of driving me nuts."

Catherine stopped walking and covered her eyes. Luke took note and pried her fingers away from her face. She was sobbing.

Without hesitation, he wrapped his long arms around her and held her tight.

"It's okay, Catherine," he said. "Everything will be okay."

"But it isn't," she said. "I'm lost. If anyone could find Trini, it should be her sister, a damn former police officer. I have so little to go on."

Luke released his strong grip and looked at her, urging her to walk toward their cottages.

Catherine walked slowly, steadily beside Luke. She hugged her chest and he slipped his hands into his jean pockets. She felt edgy about the sirens, the bright lights, seeing people dragged off, the way she once performed her duty. She wondered why Luke had come running. Or was he already there? More than she could understand, she wanted to believe him, that he was a former priest, that it was a coincidence that they lived across from one another. But what if none of it was true?

When they reached the door to her cottage, they stopped as she looked up at the brightening sky – it was nearly five in the morning; she hadn't realized how long they'd stood at the scene of the fire and arrest.

"Coffee at eleven on our rocks?" he asked.

Catherine took a deep breath and did not meet his eyes. She looked everywhere except at Luke. "I don't know," she said, "maybe not today."

Luke cocked his head to one side and looked at her. The stains from tears lingered on her face and he resisted trying to remove them. "Why?" he asked.

Catherine placed the key in her lock and turned it. "I'm just in a bad mood, Luke."

"All the more reason to have coffee with the gulls. I'll bring extra bread or something for them – I've decided it's not fair to eat in front of them."

Catherine stared at her feet and said nothing.

"Catherine," he said as his hands reached out for hers, "come on. It's going to be a great day and our place on the rocks is waiting. Let me pick you up around eleven. I'll have the coffee and other stuff all ready. What do you feel like having? I can get doughnuts, scones, whatever you want."

"Scones," she said, and then she disappeared into her cottage, closing the door behind her. She watched him go from the window, aware of those long strides across the street to his own cottage. The man was captivating, but still a mystery.

Catherine walked to the kitchen and placed water on the stove for tea then moved to her bedroom to change clothes. As she passed the window, she looked to the cottage next door and saw that the back window, which would have been the bedroom, was open. She'd never seen it open before. Catherine stepped back from her window and then edged forward so that she could continue to observe. It looked dark inside; there was no movement, nothing to see. She moved away and decided that too much of her life revolved around mystery and suspicion. She chose a fresh pair of jeans and a lightweight navy blue blouse to wear at eleven for coffee with Luke and their feathered friends. After a quick shower, Catherine drank tea and ate an orange while watching the street from her front window. There was nothing - too much of nothing.

As they sat on the rocks, less conversational than usual, Luke tossed pieces from a loaf of wheat bread to the excited gulls. Catherine took small nibbles from her scone and sipped coffee, her eyes fastened on the flurry of feathers before her and Luke's gorgeous hands offering them food. He was, she decided, the most intriguing man she'd ever met and it was going to be just awful if he turned out to be truly a fraud.

As she was deep in thought about him, Luke turned to her. "How are you feeling this morning? Last night was rough on you."

She nodded. "It was. I'm okay."

"Am I allowed to know more about you? I mean, I have the feeling that you're not totally at ease with me, and I want you to be. So if asking you questions feels like going beyond where you want us, I'll back off."

Catherine looked at Luke's handsome face. "I tend to be a careful person. It's more me than you, Luke. I doubt my own feelings quite often. I have this issue, not many people know about it, but it keeps me on my toes about everything."

"What kind of issue?" he asked turning toward her, his knees bent, his arms draped loosely over his legs.

Catherine half smiled and looked to the horizon. "I have this sensitivity to life. It's a condition called synesthesia."

"I've heard of it," he said, "but rekindle my memory."

Catherine squirmed a bit, closed her eyes, then opened them and placed her coffee cup next to her on the smooth slab of gray rock. "It affects people in different ways, but with me, I see names in color. For instance, my name is in green, like stained glass. All names appear to me in stained glass. I find beauty in things that others take for granted. I feel music. I think I feel happier and sadder than most – all the senses are heightened."

"Pain?" he asked.

"Oddly, I have a high tolerance for pain. I broke my arm when I was a kid and didn't even know it. It tends to be the emotional things I'm sensitive to." She smiled. "I find it's a good excuse for strange behavior."

Luke smiled and was quiet, digesting the information.

"I don't think I've ever met anyone who had synesthesia. Apparently it's the opposite of *anesthesia*."

"Right."

"It must be pretty cool, adding depth to wonderful

57

things."

Catherine nodded and picked up her coffee cup. "Yes, but at the same time, when my dog died years ago I was in mourning for ages. I suppose that's why finding Trini is so important to me – I can imagine what she's like and how we might enjoy being sisters."

Luke looked out to the horizon and the neon bright rim of sun nestled there.

"What kind of name is Trini? Is that it? And you must know her last name."

"I have no papers on her. All I know is Trini Bauer. Her mother's name was Helga."

"Let me see if I can help you, Catherine. I have a friend at school, a genealogy and history buff. He has an interest in name origins. I could ask him about the name Bauer – maybe we could discover more about your sister. I mean, if we had an idea of something she liked, other than the beach and drugs, you might find another path to her. I won't intervene if you tell me no, and I won't be offended. It's up to you."

Catherine looked into his beautiful eyes and longed to lean on his sturdy shoulder. "I'd be grateful for anything you might be able to add, Luke. Thank you."

They sat quietly for a while, watching the gulls swoop low and then gracefully up and around before landing with accuracy on a small wedge of rock. If only, Catherine thought, I could have their viewing ability – I could canvas this entire area in search of Trini.

"What are you doing this weekend?" Luke asked.

"More of the same."

"I'll be away," he said. "My aunt is attending a

going away party for a friend and has asked me to go with her. We'll be staying on Cape Cod tonight and tomorrow night. I'll be back on Sunday."

Catherine swallowed and felt an immediate sense of loss. "That sounds nice," she said.

Luke looked at her sweet profile and said nothing. They seemed to have a mutual appreciation of the sea and its surroundings – it was unnecessary to comment, to speak of the immense and apparent beauty.

By two-thirty, Catherine looked at her wristwatch and stood. "I suppose we should get going. What time are you meeting with your aunt?"

"We're leaving around six," he said. "What about you? What will you do with your weekend besides saturate yourself in search? You need some time out, Catherine."

She shook her head from side to side as he stood next to her. "I don't really get time off. This is my time off, having coffee on these glorious rocks. Weekends are more crowded here, maybe Trini would feel that she could more appropriately blend in. I don't know. I've only been here a few weeks and I already feel beaten down – I wish I had more to go on. It's so frustrating. Every moment that goes by is a moment in which Trini could meet with harm."

"Does she know about you?" Luke asked.

Catherine took a deep breath. "I don't know."

When they parted back at Catherine's cottage, she thought Luke might give her a hug, but he kept to a platonic move and said goodbye until Monday. Catherine stood inside her cottage feeling lonelier than she could imagine. Her mother was in Arizona, her father gone. Her sister was missing and Luke was leaving – it left her empty.

After a call to her mother, Catherine decided on a cup of tea and then a walk into town. Friday evening was always more raucous as weekenders arrived to join the regular crowd.

It was getting dark as Catherine slipped into her denim jacket. She had Trini's photo ready, determined to be more assertive about asking people if they'd seen her.

After buying herself another raspberry lime-rickey, Catherine walked up to three young women, holding bottles of beer, not looking old enough to consume them. She excused herself for interrupting their laughter and showed them the photo of Trini. They had never seen her before. Catherine showed the picture to several other groups with no indication of recognition. As she started to walk toward her cottage, someone stepped out in front of her. The action startled Catherine as she looked at the opened shirt and bare chest of a tough looking character.

"What's that you got that you're showin' around," he asked.

Catherine pulled the photo from her purse and showed him. "Have you seen this girl?" she asked.

He looked for a long time then smiled and laughed. "Sure. She comes here all the time. Matter of fact, I'm expectin' her tonight."

"Are you sure?" Catherine asked with a pounding heart.

"Sure as I'm standin' here with you, Sweetheart."

Catherine was unnerved. She wasn't confident that

she could believe him, but what if she could? What if Trini just showed up and the search was over?

"I have a place just a few doors up. Would you care to join me?" he asked with a bow.

Catherine disliked his type, but this was the first lead she'd had on her sister. How could she pass it up?

He started to walk slowly and turned to see if she was following. She was. At a dark, ramshackle dwelling, he stopped. He again turned and looked at Catherine, his eyes traveling over her from head to toe. He inserted a key into the lock and opened the door to a cluttered room. Catherine stepped inside and thought the place reeked of beer and stale cigarettes. She was pretty sure this had been a mistake, but she was there.

"Sit down," he said as he closed and locked the door. He flipped a switch and a dingy overhead light attempted to illuminate the room.

"I'm okay," Catherine said, as she remained standing.

"I don't recall *inviting* you to sit. I *told* you to sit," he said gruffly.

Catherine looked at him then sat down on a dirty looking chair.

"When did you last see her?" Catherine asked.

He laughed. "Not in a while," he said, "but you and me got each other. We don't need her."

Catherine's heart pounded. "You said you knew her. You said she might be coming in later."

He laughed again. "Yah, well I say a lot of things."

Catherine stood and walked toward the door. He stood in her way. She placed her hand on the doorknob and he forced her to the ground. Her training kicked in.

She grabbed his thick leg and switched positions with him – now he was on the floor and she was standing, her teeth gritted as she glared at him in semi-darkness. She flipped a switch to further illuminate the dingy, dirty room.

"Don't even think about messing with me," she said. "I have a black belt and if I need to, I'll make you regret your measly life." Catherine surprised herself with the ferocity she felt and had the strength to put it into action. "I'll hurt you," she threatened.

The grubby man looked at her and rubbed his shoulder. "Get the hell out," he said as if he'd swallowed gravel.

Catherine backed up to the door, keeping her eyes on him, then she turned the handle. "No problem," she said and was gone.

Outside in the fresh air, she could smell the mixture of salt breeze and popcorn and she shivered at what could have occurred. She looked at her watch and saw that it was after two in the morning. She walked back to the cottage, checking behind her every few seconds. Inside her own small abode, she locked the door, slipped down onto the sofa and cried. Not so much for what she'd endured, but for once again finding a dead end to her search for Trini.

On Saturday morning, Catherine showered, dressed and made her way to town for coffee. She thought that if she encountered that miserable character again, she just might slow him down. She bought her hot coffee and a blueberry muffin then walked back to the cottage. At ten, she thought about going to the rocks, but it wouldn't be the same without Luke. She glanced over at the green cottage next door and then out to the street watching the passers-by. At noon, she went out to her car and drove to the rocky area. She sat there, her eyes on the sea and the gulls. *Where do they sleep?* She wished Luke was there, but it would be Monday before he'd be back.

Catherine sipped her coffee and thought about her father. She wanted to be angry with him for having an affair while her parents were separated, but with Trini as a result, she found it hard to deny the union which had resulted in a new life. Babies weren't mistakes, no matter what.

She wished she didn't remember the argument her parents had the night before he left. She'd never seen her parents do anything more than bicker, but this night, things had been different. She saw their anger, heard their furious voices and she was afraid. Then she saw her mother take a pink slipper and hit Catherine's father across the face. That act of violence startled Catherine. She'd never seen anything like that before. Two days later, her father pulled her aside and explained that he wouldn't be living there anymore. When Catherine tried to take his hand to ask why, he pushed his young daughter away and said nothing. Catherine vividly recalled the slipper to his face and she was certain that this incident had everything to do with his leaving. When he came back months later, it wasn't the same. Catherine kept expecting something else bad – she listened for sounds of discontent – she heard nothing and life went on.

Later in the afternoon, Catherine drove through town and to all the surrounding side streets. She was vigilant about every detail, opened doors, closed windows, shops which might attract a young woman, if only for necessities. She drove back to her own place around five and, exhausted, thought about what someone twenty-two and trying to be inconspicuous might do with herself. If with a friend, she might stay inside, out of sight. If longing to get out on a Saturday night, she might don a disguise, a different color to her hair, a different style. Catherine started to think about every possibility. She would go out after dark when things in town started to jump; she would examine as closely as she could the face of every young woman in sight.

At nine o'clock, the deep blue sky dotted with hundreds of visible stars, Catherine wore an ankle-length skirt in shades of blue and green and her black shirt. She allowed her hair to hang carelessly, as if she'd come from the beach with no thought to style. She was pretty – she turned heads, but Catherine kept walking, sauntering through the streets, not feeling as confident as her stride might suggest.

She decided, too, that Trini might not be in a group of girls where attention might be more focused on her – perhaps she would go out alone, prepared to meet her needs unnoticed. At a sidewalk café, Catherine watched a girl with a dark brown braid – she watched her from the back, aware that she seemed to be alone as she purchased a bagel and stuffed it in her purse. Catherine could see where someone in hiding would do that, taking food with her. The girl could have several food items in that large purse, in preparation for staying out of sight. When the girl turned, Catherine was disappointed to see that there was no resemblance to Trini.

It was near midnight; the beach strip was flooded with open bars and obviously inebriated people roaming the streets. Catherine felt drained. She'd stared into so many young faces, none of them belonging to her sister. She spoke to no one – people were coupled up or amidst a crowd – the opportunity to show the photo hadn't presented itself, not without drawing unwanted attention. Everything she did had to be with caution, keeping in mind that to put the spotlight on herself was to put it on Trini as well.

Catherine walked toward her cottage and at the edge of the strip turned around and just looked at the mass of people and the bright colored lights. Everywhere she looked, there were red neon open signs, lights advertising beer, pizza, all sorts of options to add fun, food and games to life. It had never held appeal to Catherine, but she could easily understand why it drew in so many young people and others who lived on the edge.

She turned again and in-minutes was back at the cottage. She inserted the key in the lock and glanced quickly toward Luke's place. No car, one dim light on inside, no Luke. Resigned to spend the rest of the long night alone, and facing the next day on her own, she sighed and walked inside, locking the door behind her. She leaned her back and hands against the door and looked around the dull and dingy room. She wanted to leave this space, the entire area, but she could not – not without Trini.

Catherine slipped out of her clothes and into a

shower. The cascading water felt soothing, she stayed there longer than usual. When the hot water began to turn tepid and then cool, she stopped the shower and dried herself before changing into a pair of jersey pants and a t-shirt. She made tea and then sat in the wooden rocker until after two in the morning. At that point, she walked to her bedroom and lay across the bed, falling asleep within minutes.

Just before dawn, Catherine was wakened by the slamming of a door and then a car's engine. She looked out to see that the man from the green cottage was leaving. She wondered what his story was – everyone had one. Catherine went to the kitchen and made tea, then walked to the front window, her eyes drawn to Luke's driveway and the lonely, empty space. It was Sunday – now what?

She walked to town and found it was a calm, sleepy place. A few people passed her carrying a newspaper and coffee, but no one walked with a sense of purpose, everyone seemed tired, slow. Catherine bought herself a coffee and muffin, then a plastic bag of day-old bread for the gulls. She walked back to the cottage. She didn't go inside – she went to her car and drove to the beautiful rocky shore. Several others had the same idea. Catherine walked to the place she and Luke had claimed as their own and sat down. She tossed small pieces of bread to the gulls then ate her muffin in about five bites. She lingered over the coffee, her eyes to the horizon. The immense tranquility of the vast ocean calmed her heart and spirit.

One year ago, she thought her life was settled. She was a police officer with no knowledge of a sister.

Everything was upside down now – no answers, no clues, no planned life.

Chapter Five

Sunday had been quiet and Monday couldn't come too soon. Catherine admitted to herself that she missed seeing Luke. Even the fact that his driveway was empty troubled her.

When she moved the lace curtain to the side and looked out at five in the morning, she smiled and took a deep breath. Luke was back. With a definite lift to her spirit and in her bare feet, Catherine walked to the kitchen and made tea. She would wait until nine-thirty or ten when she'd knock on his door to see if eleven on the rocks would work. Until then, she would shower, walk to town and carouse the shops showing Trini's photo. She would keep her eyes on all young women - and then she'd walk back to the cottage.

No one Catherine encountered in town had the slightest resemblance to Trini and no one acknowledged ever seeing her at all. Day after day of discouragement was all Catherine could account for, except that she knew through her police work, it would only take one sighting, one moment, then Trini could be within arm's reach. Nothing would deter Catherine – she would continue her search.

Back at her cottage by ten-fifteen, Catherine was fishing for her key when she heard Luke call to her.

"Are we on the rocks at eleven?" he asked halfway

across the street.

Catherine turned and smiled. "Sounds good."

Luke walked up to her, so close that she thought he might touch her. "Will you ride with me or would you prefer to drive on your own?"

"I'll meet you there," she said. "In fact, I've just come from town; I have cranberry corn muffins. Interested?"

"Sure. I'll pick up coffee and meet you on the rocks in about thirty minutes."

Catherine inserted the key into the lock then turned to face him. "Okay, and I have bread for the gulls."

"Perfect," he said with a lingering smile. "I'll see you shortly then."

It seemed for a few moments that neither of them wanted to move, but when Catherine opened the door and walked inside her cottage, Luke backed up a few steps, turned and walked toward his place.

Later, he sat close to Catherine on the rocks and said, "Tell me what you did this weekend."

Catherine opened the paper bag and took out the loaf of bread for the gulls and then the muffins. "I didn't do much," she said, "more of the same, always hoping for a glimpse of Trini."

"I was concerned you might venture out at night," he said. "The strip is loaded with some pretty unsavory characters."

Catherine nodded, not mentioning how she'd fallen for lines from the thug who led her to his shack and his bad intentions.

Luke looked at her and then touched her arm so lightly it almost felt like a breeze. "What happened there?" he asked pointing to a lengthy bruise.

Catherine looked down at her arm and was surprised to see black and blue skin from her elbow to her wrist. She didn't reply.

"Catherine, what happened? Did you take a fall?"

She looked at Luke and decided to admit the truth. "I did something stupid."

"Like what?"

Catherine was quiet and looked down at the bag in her hands.

"Catherine," he touched her hand, "tell me what happened. Who did this?"

"I fell," she said, and then she relayed what actually happened.

Luke seemed horrified. "Catherine, for God's sake, why would you do such a thing? You're a former police officer; that must have been in the training."

Catherine swallowed and looked out to sea before her eyes met his. "I did everything we tell the public not to do. I was desperate – all I could think of was finding my sister. This was the only hope I had and I was stupidly willing to take the chance."

"How did you get away from him?" Luke asked still shaken.

"When he was a little more sober and reached for me, I grabbed his ankle and knocked him down. I told him I had a black belt and I'd hurt him."

Luke laughed. "That was good thinking. You don't really have a black belt, right?"

Catherine's lips spread into a wide grin. "Oh yes, I do, so watch it."

The expression on Luke's face made Catherine

laugh. "You've really been in hiding behind those dark robes of yours, haven't you? Women today are not helpless little waifs who get tossed on a man's shoulder and carried off to his cave. We have opportunities to learn about being defensive."

Luke looked away from Catherine and then back at her pretty face and her hair being tossed in the wind.

"You keep surprising me," he said. "You don't look like a police officer and you don't look like you'd have a black belt."

Catherine smiled as she looked at his intensely dark eyes. "So, what do I look like then? Some frail little thing who faints at the first sign of trouble?"

"You," he said as his eyes met hers with sincerity, "look a lot like every man's dream."

Catherine's smile vanished. She hadn't expected that reply and wasn't sure what to say or do in return.

Luke noticed he'd made her uncomfortable. He looked out to sea and then back at her profile, her eyes squinting against the ocean glare. "Look, I know you have mirrors in that little cottage. It can't be surprising to hear me utter complimentary words about you. I'd bet lots of men have expressed similar if not the exact same sentiments."

Catherine squirmed on the flat width of rock and kept her eyes averted from Luke.

"Catherine," he interrupted her thoughts, "are you mad at me for noticing you?"

She was confused for a moment about exactly what he implied. Did he mean noticing her at the cottage, or that he meant simply noticing her as a woman? One urge was to melt into him, and the other was to keep

71

him at arm's length.

"Hey," he said as he leaned a little closer, "what's going on here? Come on, give a guy a break. I'm rusty at this stuff. Take mercy on a poor, old priest."

Catherine looked to a distant island and then at Luke. "You're not poor, you're not old, and if you're telling me the truth, you're not a priest."

He started to smile and then didn't. "You doubt me?"

Catherine looked away for a moment and then back at his handsome face. "You told me you were a fraud. It's been said that when someone shows you who they are, believe them the first time."

Luke looked away from her and then back. "Boy, I guess I'm going to live to regret that stupid statement. Look, I *am* a fraud, to my aunt and a handful of her friends. And quite honestly, Catherine, I haven't had the opportunity to show you who I am, yet."

He stood, picked up the trash, then walked slowly away.

When Catherine turned to look where he had gone, he was nowhere in sight. She stood and then with a last glance toward the sea, turned again and walked toward her car, wondering if she'd just ruined the most interesting relationship of her life.

Back at her own cottage, she looked across to Luke's place and noted that his car was not there. She swallowed back tears as she entered the small, stuffy space and locked the door behind her. Her instinct was to make tea, but she didn't want any. She paced to and from the window and then she sat down in the rocking chair. She'd longed to see Luke after his weekend away, and now it could be gone forever.

When Catherine woke up at four in the afternoon, she heard a car door and voices next door. She walked to her bedroom window, standing back a bit as she watched. She saw the same male, a light-haired man in his early to mid-twenties take a dark-haired girl by the arm as he led her to his car. She looked drunk or drugged. This was Catherine's first sighting of a female from that house – she'd seen the man multiple times, and now what was he doing with her? She looked like she needed medical attention. Secured in the car, they drove off toward town and Catherine hoped it was to see a doctor. This place was rampant with tough living people. The thought of Trini staying in town, hiding and ever finding happiness there, bewildered Catherine.

When it was dark enough to entice the evening crowd out onto the streets, Catherine dressed in jeans and an Army green jersey. She walked to town, blending in with the inhabitants and tourists, eating a soft pretzel as her eyes traveled over each face. Just one instant, one glance of Trini would make all of this worthwhile. To know that she was safe, to be able to speak to her, to tell her that they were sisters, would mean so much. Catherine used the back of her hand to wipe away stray tears as she walked. Each step had the possibility of finding Trini.

At a shop where she purchased an iced coffee, Catherine took the photo from her purse and asked the young waitress if she'd seen this girl.

"Why?" the waitress asked with suspicion in her voice. "Why do you want to know?"

"She's a friend," Catherine said. "I know she

comes here, I was hoping to surprise her with a visit."

The waitress looked doubtful. "I can't help you," she said.

Catherine looked at the girl who seemed about Trini's age. She knew the girl was lying by her attitude.

"It's important," Catherine continued. "I have something for her and I know she'd be grateful to you for helping me."

The girl looked at Catherine and walked away tending to other customers. Catherine backed out of the small stand and walked on. People there knew Trini, but they weren't talking. She understood that that's what young people did – they concealed information and stayed mum about one another's business.

Catherine walked through town and back again, her eyes moving left to right, at times thinking that she had found a resemblance, then determining that she had not. It kept her on edge and she assumed that must be how firemen lived, always waiting for that sudden and unexpected alarm.

The rank odor of beer seemed to float through the streets and although she enjoyed an occasional brew with pizza, she found the strong aroma almost sickening in the summer heat.

Before midnight, she walked back toward her cottage, bumping into more than one drunk as she tried to avoid groups shuffling or staggering along together.

"Catherine," she heard Luke's voice as she began to insert the key into her door's lock.

She turned to face him, the dim light from the streetlight illuminating his face.

"I'm sorry," he said. "I was out of line today."

74

Catherine could feel warm tears cascading down her face. Everything was such a mess. Her father was dead, her mother had bolted for Arizona, her best friend had moved twelve hundred miles away, and Trini was nowhere. But it was Luke. Luke had entered and taunted her heart and left her feeling empty without him. In this whole miserable mess, it was Luke whose absence now made her cry.

Catherine turned the key in the lock and walked inside. She stepped to the right indicating that Luke was invited in. He stuffed his hands into trouser pockets, walked inside and looked around as she closed the door.

Catherine smoothed the tears away and asked if he'd like tea. "I don't keep any alcohol here," she said. "And I buy my coffee ready made in town. Sorry."

Luke smiled. "It's okay. I like tea."

Catherine dropped her purse into a chair and walked to the tiny kitchen. Luke followed, watching her. She poured fresh water into a kettle and placed it on the small stovetop then took two mugs from a cupboard and placed a teabag in each one.

"I don't have milk or sugar either," she said.

"I drink it black like my coffee."

Catherine sighed and leaned against the sink area as they waited for the kettle to sing. They were quiet. The whistle broke their silence. Catherine turned the stove off and poured steaming water into their mugs. She carried them into the front room and left the mugs on a table to steep and cool.

"Sit down," she invited.

Luke hesitated then sat down on one end of the sofa. Catherine sat in her rocker.

"I suppose you went looking for your sister again tonight," he said.

Catherine nodded.

"Any sign of her at all?"

"I showed her picture to a young waitress where I buy coffee. I know she recognized Trini, but she wouldn't say anything about her. I understand these kids, I know they don't want to rat anyone out, but it makes my search so freaking impossible. All I can do is continue to look. One of these times, I'm going to see her."

Luke reached for his tea and took a sip before placing it back down to cool.

"Does your place look as bad as this one?" Catherine asked.

Luke smiled. "Afraid so." He was silent for a few moments and seemed to sense that Catherine was mentally and physically exhausted. He watched as she sat forward, reached for her tea and took a few sips. She held the mug in her hands, the warmth was soothing.

"When I came to your door tonight," he said, "what made you cry? Was it me?"

Catherine looked at her tea and then at Luke. "Yeah, I guess so."

Luke was quiet as he studied her tousled hair and beautiful face. "It wasn't my intention to make you cry, Catherine."

"I know."

Luke sat back and smiled. "Well, this is awkward. I said the wrong thing this morning and I made the girl cry tonight. On a scale of one to ten, I'm a zero at relationships."

Catherine looked at him. "It's not you. It's everything. I feel so disconnected. I have no job, my mother has moved two thousand miles away, one of my best friends moved to Chicago last year, and another friend is pretty sure she's going to marry this sweet guy from Canada and live up there. I feel like a guppy in the ocean."

Luke laughed quietly. "That's quite an image," he said, "when you consider the sharks in the sea." He leaned forward for his mug of tea and took a few swallows.

Catherine crossed one leg over the other and shifted in the rocking chair.

"May I ask you something a little personal?" he said.

She looked at him and nodded. "I guess so."

"You asked if I'd ever been with someone, with a woman. I told you about college, before the seminary. How about you? Has there been a love in your life, or many?"

Catherine's eyes examined the dark tea and then she looked up at Luke. "I had the same boyfriend from the time I was about fifteen until three years ago. We met, we became best friends, and years, literally years into the friendship we finally decided to have what we called a grown-up relationship."

Luke was quiet for a few moments then asked, "What happened with him? Is he still part of your life?"

Catherine smiled sadly. "He'll always be part of my life."

Luke put his half-full mug of tea down and stared at his hands before asking, "Where is he? Is he the friend who moved away?"

Catherine shook her head slowly. "He died. He was a racecar driver. I always feared he'd be killed flying around some racetrack, but four years ago, he told me he was having dizzy spells and his handwriting became difficult. I thought it might be blood pressure, something for which he'd take a pill and all would be fine again. It turns out that Riley had brain cancer. Twenty-five years old, brain cancer. Less than a year later, he died."

"Oh my God," Luke said quietly. "That's tragic. All the times as a priest that I heard similar things about loss and young people, I was never sure what I could say to bring comfort. Maybe there's nothing. I'm so sorry, Catherine."

"It still seems impossible that he's gone," she said, "but after that, after losing him, that's when I decided to become a police officer. I needed a change in my life. I knew he'd laugh if he was watching from some lofty cloud – he'd never have suspected I'd go in for such a career."

Luke was quiet for a few minutes then told Catherine that something had gone on in the green cottage next to hers.

"Like what? What happened over there?" she asked.

"I don't really know, but around ten o'clock, a car pulled into the driveway. I'd just gotten back with a pizza and was going into my own place. I saw the fellow who seems to live there half dragging a young girl into the house. She was resisting, but then she cried and hugged him. He took her inside and that was it. I thought about calling the police, but then I wondered what I'd say to them. It was like a young couple having a spat."

"Could you see the girl? Do you know what she looked like?"

"All I had was the streetlight, but she was dark-haired and desperately thin."

"That's the girl I saw earlier. She seemed affected by drugs or something. My urge is always to intervene, but in what way? I hate that Trini has been living with this sort of thing. I saw it often as part of my job in the patrol car, but it never gets to be okay."

Luke scanned Catherine's serene face as she closed her eyes for a few moments. "I should go," he said as he stood. "It's late and you're tired. Coffee on the rocks at eleven?"

She opened her eyes and stood, walking with him toward the door. "Yes, that sounds nice."

"I'll bring the coffee stuff," he said.

"And the bread for the gulls?"

"And the bread for the gulls. Goodnight, Catherine."

"Goodnight," she said, and then he was gone.

Catherine sat down again in the rocking chair and thought about the waitress who was obviously hiding whatever she knew of Trini. Catherine had no power to insist that the girl come forward with whatever she knew. It made her wonder how many people in that small beach community knew where Trini was and would reveal nothing. If only she could convince them that she meant no harm – she wasn't the police.

After stretching and feeling that she needed some

rest, Catherine walked to the small bedroom, looked toward the green cottage, which was dark and still, then lay down in a fetal position where she fell asleep on top of the covers.

During the night she woke and listened, thinking she had heard a thud outside. When she heard nothing more, she turned back to her pillow and slept until daylight.

Without the use of a washing machine, and not wanting to haul her laundry into town, Catherine hand-washed underwear, jeans, three jerseys and a blouse. To meet Luke at eleven, she showered then selected a pair of cuffed chino shorts and a loose fitting dark green shirt. She brushed her hair and decided to pull it back into a ponytail.

When he saw her sitting on the rocks as he approached, he stopped and smiled. She could have been taken for about thirteen.

Catherine turned around and saw him. He was all in black again. She smiled and waved but was acutely aware of the fact that this was no ordinary man. Luke had been a priest and her bet was that he was good at his work.

He walked toward her, carefully choosing his steps until he was sharing the large, flat rock where they usually sat.

"Hi," he said as he passed the brown bag to Catherine. "We have blueberry muffins with our coffee today, and the gulls have honey-wheat bread." He sat down closer to Catherine than usual, yet not touching.

Catherine looked into the bag. After taking the loaf of bread out first, she carefully lifted a blueberry muffin and handed it to Luke then she took her own from the bag, leaving the coffee at the bottom. "I'm starved," she said. "This muffin smells so good."

They ate and drank their coffee companionably while tossing pieces of bread to the waiting gulls.

After a short while, Catherine's hair ribbon loosened and strands of her long hair began to cling to the sides of her face and neck. She pulled the ribbon off and held her hair in place. Luke noticed and moved closer to her asking her to turn her head away from him. Skillfully, his fingers entwined her auburn hair into a braid, once again, fastening it with her own hair, and then the ribbon.

"There," he said. "You're all set."

Catherine looked at him and then moved her hand to feel the braid and the part of her neck where Luke's fingers had brushed against her skin.

"Thank you," she said softly.

Luke smiled then asked, "What color is my name?"

Catherine hesitated, not understanding at first, and then she remembered that she'd told him about synesthesia. "It's a heavenly shade of pale blue," she said.

Luke laughed. "Is that 'heavenly shade' because of my former vocation?"

"It has nothing to do with it," she said. "It's just your color."

"And yours is green?" he asked.

"Yes, green."

They sat quietly for a few moments when Luke said, "You're lucky, you know."

81

"I know," she said.

Lapses of silent time didn't seem awkward for Catherine and Luke. She liked that they could sit on the rocks watching the surf and gulls without words, and yet, there was so much she would have liked to ask. His choice of the priesthood made her wonder – what drew him in and what caused him to leave? He seemed so logical, so well put together.

"What's next?" Luke asked. "Do you have a plan if searching for your sister here doesn't work?"

Catherine looked up at the cloud-dotted sky and then back at the sea. "I came here hoping I'd see her. I knew there was a possibility I wouldn't, simply because of the two men who are also looking for her. She's obviously hiding. If I don't find her here, I don't know what else to do. I've made copies of her picture and sent it to every shelter I could find listed, even out of state. The problem is, if someone wants to conceal themselves, they can stay inside, they can change their looks. I may have passed Trini a dozen times already. Sometimes I'm angry with my father, and that's unreasonable because he's gone. Instead of being sad over losing him, I'm kind of mad at him."

Luke looked into Catherine's blue eyes. "Remember when I told you about a friend at school who might be of help?"

"Did you find something out, Luke?"

"It's not a lot, but he called me this morning. He's discovered a Helga Bauer who had spent time in this area as a nanny, right around the time that your sister would have been conceived. Apparently she returned to Germany pregnant. The bad part is she passed away a few years ago."

Catherine's heartbeat became noticeably faster. She sat up straight and looked at Luke, her hand grasping his right arm. "Are there other family members in Germany? Maybe someone has had contact with Trini."

"He tried to find out more. It seems that Helga was an orphan – no one seems connected to her. It's a dead end, Catherine, but at least it's understandable why Trini came here. Maybe all she had was her young friends and maybe your father."

"Luke, am I supposed to accept that Trini's whereabouts have gone to the grave with my dad?"

They were both silent again for a long time, their eyes moving with the gulls, the waves, the wind blowing stringy lengths of seaweed across the rocks.

"Tonight," Luke said, "let me walk into town with you. We can both look; maybe I'd see something you missed. When we've exhausted our search, I'd like to take you to Ricardo's for dinner. It's relaxing there. I think you need a rest from this search now and then. What do you think?"

Catherine sighed as quietly as she could. Giving up a full night's search was going to be difficult, but Ricardo's with Luke held appeal.

"I really didn't bring clothes with me for a place like Ricardo's, especially night-time apparel."

"How about if we buy you something in town tonight? That would also give us a good excuse to show Trini's picture in that shop."

Later, Catherine walked alongside Luke as they blended in with the throngs of people. At a shop where there were mostly t-shirts and bathing gear, Catherine saw a rack of dresses. One of them was black, a light fabric with a fitted top and free-flowing ankle-length skirt. Tiny white pearl buttons graced the bodice.

Luke smiled and nodded his approval. "I like it," he said.

"Because it's black?" she teased.

"Because it suits you."

"Well, it's nearly ten. I think we should head back to the cottages and get ready for dinner. I'm starved."

"Me too," he said. "Let's go."

Luke insisted that he drive Catherine to Ricardo's. He wore dark gray slacks and a pure white short-sleeved shirt open at the throat. Catherine wore her black dress with a pair of black sandals. They were a couple who earned a second look – striking.

Seated near a window overlooking a seawall and garden, Catherine took a deep breath and smiled as Luke sat across from her.

"I needed this more than I knew," she admitted.

Close to eleven o'clock, they ordered light meals, salads with curried chicken, and each of them decided on a glass of Pinot Grigio. They lingered there watching the swirling tide then decided on a brief walk before heading back to their own places.

"I think I could get used to this," Luke said as he walked with his hands in his trouser pockets.

Catherine smiled in the semi-darkness with firm sand beneath her feet. "It's beautiful here. It aggravates me though that just a mile or two down the street, people like my sister live in such inferior conditions. It's a class shock," she said. "There's this wonderful place that everyone should have access to, and then there's the beach strip. It seems unfair."

"Life is unfair," Luke said as they walked. "We don't have to like it, but the imbalance is everywhere."

"Sometimes I feel like a socialist," Catherine said. "I want everyone to have a decent home, the basics."

Luke looked at her profile in the moonlight. She was so much more than physically beautiful. Catherine stopped walking and turned to Luke, which took him by surprise.

"Were you in love with that girl in college?"

Luke stood motionless and then he smiled. "That girl," he said. "No, I liked her, we were friends; we had fun, but love, no."

"So you've never been in love?"

"I was pretty hung up on a girl in eighth grade, but she had eyes for another. I was crushed."

Reversing their direction to head back toward his car, Luke walked with Catherine at his side. "But my mother said something pretty significant to my tender, teenaged ears. She said it was more important who you loved than who loved you. We can't help what other people think and feel, but it's very telling who we care for. Do you think she had it right?"

"I don't know. What was the girl like? Was she nice?"

Luke smiled. "Actually, she was *very* nice."

Catherine nodded. "It sounds like your mother was right."

The conversation, light as it was intended, left Catherine feeling a little envious.

Chapter Six

Days went by with similar routines. Catherine met Luke on the rocks for coffee, scones or muffins, bread for the seagulls, and sunglasses when the glare became penetrating.

On Friday, Catherine looked at Luke as they ate raspberry scones. "Are you going away again this weekend?"

Luke looked at Catherine's profile and asked, "Would you miss me if I went?"

Catherine took the sunglasses from her eyes and looked at Luke with a sly smile. "You know, you're pretty savvy for a priest."

"What is that supposed to mean?" he asked with a nudge to her elbow.

"I probably shouldn't be too surprised – after all, you were a man first. However, you are always ready with the questions and answers. It's not like you're rusty, or dense."

"Well, thanks," Luke said, and they laughed.

After a few quiet moments Catherine folded her sunglasses into her hands and looked at him. "What really made you leave? You told me you had come to realize that you were a priest for all the wrong reasons – I don't think I understand what that means."

Luke's expression became solemn. "It's been close

to two years and I still feel like I abandoned something important. The reasons I left were my own. I really was looking for a space where I could find comfort – it's supposed to be the other way around. I think I realized early on that I'd made a mistake. And then, not long into my first parish assignment, I met a charming couple. They invited me to dinner at their home and first-rate restaurants. They gave me expensive gifts. I began to realize that she had a crush on me, which made things tense. Then I went away for a weekend, they knew I was taking a break and where. I walked into the lobby of a small hotel where I was staying and was greeted by the husband of the couple. I asked where his wife was and he frankly told me that he was there alone. I found it odd, until he offered to buy me drinks and dinner. I made excuses why I couldn't comply, but late that night, he knocked on my door."

"Wait a minute," Catherine said, "are you saying that they *both* had an interest in you?"

Luke bit his lower lip and looked out to the green-gray sea. "That's what I'm saying."

Catherine was quiet. She swallowed a sip of coffee then looked toward where several gulls circled before landing on rocks below.

"Did you think of requesting a transfer?"

"I did, but instead I decided it was time to be true to myself. My heart wasn't in it. I respect the priesthood enough to know when I have the ability to be good at my work and when I need to call it quits. I began to realize, too, that I want a life with someone, a family of my own. It's pretty lonely being a priest. I admire the men who handle it well."

87

Catherine placed her sunglasses back over her eyes. She sat quietly, her thoughts of Luke struggling with what he thought was right and what he thought too difficult to achieve. He was the kind of man she'd have liked as a priest, but he was also the kind of man she could not get out of her mind. She'd been attracted to him from the first moment, even when seeing that white patch at his throat.

"You asked about the weekend," Luke said. "I'll be here. My aunt left for North Carolina. No more pretenses."

Catherine's heart nearly leapt out of her chest. "Does that mean you no longer have a reason to stay in Rhode Island?"

Luke looked her directly in the eyes. "I have a reason."

When he didn't look away, Catherine felt lightheaded. Was he telling her in his own way that he felt something for her? This wasn't just a way to pass time while seeing his godmother for a few weeks? She wanted to hug him, to hold him so close that their hearts would be beating against one another. This was crazy, she thought, to have fallen, no, stumbled, right into love. What was there about this Luke Renoir?

"It's after two," she said as she scrambled to her feet. "I should get going. I'm the eternal optimist, always hoping for a glimpse of Trini."

"Any time for a drink or dinner later? Or would you like company on your walk through town?" Luke asked as he stood, gathering their paper cups and brown bag.

"Sure," she said. "We could walk around town and

maybe have a drink there where we might catch a glimpse of Trini. We might even see two suspicious looking young men together. We could follow them. I'd feel better about doing that with a buddy."

"What time is good?" he asked.

"After eight - I think the dark brings hide-a-ways out; at least I can hope."

They walked back to their cars and after Catherine slipped behind her wheel, Luke closed the door and said he'd see her at eight.

Catherine spent the afternoon taking a brief walk into town, showering and calling her mother in Arizona. She didn't tell her that she was actively searching for Trini – that had been a tough subject. There was no sense reviving sad memories regarding her father's union with another woman.

By seven-thirty, Catherine had changed into a knee-length chino skirt and a long sleeved white blouse. With her white sandals on her bare feet, she was ready to go. She looked out through the lace-curtained window toward Luke's cottage. His car was there; he'd be stopping by for her soon.

Catherine sat down in the rocking chair and thought about the weeks spent in the small cottage; nothing before had ever made her so tense. Everything she did could affect Trini or lead to her. She sensed her nearby and wondered if Trini knew of her mother's death. She must, and perhaps that was the reason that Trini followed in her mother's footsteps, becoming an au pair.

There was so much to consider and so few clues as to where the beautiful little blonde could be hiding. It was Catherine's great wish that she could find, know, and love her little sister just six years her junior. How unfortunate to grow up not knowing that you have a sibling of the same gender.

Just before eight, Luke knocked on Catherine's door. She jumped up to answer it and saw his smiling face. She stood back and looked at him thinking that his color sense was remarkable. He wore chocolate brown slacks and a brown and tan symmetrically patterned shirt with a collar. He looked like a male model.

"You look nice," he said. "I like you in white."

Catherine grabbed her purse and keys, locking the front door as they stepped outside. "But you like me in black as well."

"I like you in anything," he said, and Catherine's heart tumbled.

In town, they walked with no particular plan. They had decided to visually take in as many faces as possible, to poke in and out of shops. After an hour of walking, they stopped at a café Catherine had not been to and ordered appetizers and a glass of wine. They lingered there, watching people come and go. At one point, Catherine caught a glimpse of a young blonde with a braid. When the girl turned, it became obvious that she was not Trini and that there were two braids, not one.

By eleven, they were meandering through town again. Luke pointed to some artistic looking kites and mentioned that he loved them, and that maybe they should go flying them on the grassy area near their rocks.

"We can give those seagulls a run for their

money," he said smiling.

"I'm game," Catherine said as she walked into the shop and up to a red dragon kite. Luke laughed at her choice and then chose a huge black bat for himself.

"I'll race you tomorrow morning," Catherine said. "My fire-breathing dragon against your blood-thirsty black bat."

Luke laughed again. "Sounds like a deal. Let's get them."

With their kites tightly rolled in their hands, they made their way through town one more time and then headed back to the row of cottages. When they arrived at Catherine's, there was a small package sitting on her steps. There was no name, no address, just a package tied in brown paper and white string.

"What the heck is this?" she asked as she bent to pick it up.

Luke's first reaction was that she should probably put it down. "It could be a drug delivery," he said.

"But why to me? I don't know anyone here, and even if I did, I don't use drugs. This is curious. I wonder what's inside."

They stood, each of them with their eyes on the plainly wrapped parcel.

"If you're intent on opening that, I'd like to be with you for the unveiling."

Catherine opened her door and invited Luke inside. They placed their kites on the sofa.

"I'll get a knife," she said. When she returned from the kitchen, Luke held the package as she cut the string.

Carefully, slowly, she pulled at the coarse brown paper until a small, plain white box was revealed. They looked at one another, and then Catherine lifted the top. Inside, there was crumpled up newsprint. Catherine moved her fingers, cautiously peeling the paper away until she saw an ornate necklace. She lifted it and although she thought it was pretty, it was definitely not her type of jewelry. It had stones to emulate diamonds and sapphires – it was gaudy, yet with its intricate gold chain, striking. Catherine held it high against a light so that she and Luke could better see the details.

"Wow, some admirer you must have," Luke said as he touched the jewelry.

"This looks like ten-cent store stuff," Catherine said. "And I can't imagine who would have left it here."

"What about that guy you encountered last week? Did he follow you home by any chance?"

"I don't see how he could have without me noticing. This is crazy." Catherine placed the necklace back in the box and left it on the coffee table. "It's probably a mistake," she said. "With no address on the package, I can see how this might happen. I have no one who would leave this for me."

Luke asked if she was going to be okay alone – did she want him to stay.

"I'm fine," she said. "I'm actually tired. Going with you tonight made the task more relaxing – it was nice to have you tag-a-long. Thank you, Luke."

He reached out and hugged her lightly. "Tomorrow? Eleven on the rocks?"

Catherine reluctantly released him and said that she would bring the coffee, muffins and bread for the morning. Luke took his bat-shaped kite and left.

After he had crossed the street to his own place,

Catherine closed and locked the door. She glanced at the piece of costume jewelry and walked to her bedroom where she changed into soft jersey pajamas. Her room was lit only by pale moonlight as she looked next door to see that the windows were dark. It interested her to see how people lived. The car belonging to the young man in that cottage was not flashy or cheap. He had the look of a college kid, yet what was he doing there with a girl who seemed to be in very frail shape? Catherine hung her clothes on a hanger then walked out to the front room and her rocker. Her evening with Luke had been made so much nicer than walking the streets alone. She smiled as she turned out the light and loved the way the moonlight sifted through the lace on the window. She understood that most would miss this intricate glimmer of light; this was a gift to her from synesthesia. Ordinary objects became extraordinary.

The remainder of the night found her there in the rocking chair, sleeping restlessly, but content in that space. In the morning, she would again scan faces and shops. She would buy coffee, muffins, and day-old bread for the winged acrobats of the sea. Catherine smiled thinking of being with Luke again, and their kites flying high at the grassy area near where they parked their cars. Being with him was fun.

When Catherine woke up at seven, birds outside her kitchen window were chirping and singing. She wished that she had birdseed. She tossed a crumbled slice of bread from the back door - she watched – they ate.

She made tea, changed into jeans and a jersey, then

walked into the front room to look through the curtained window. Luke's car was gone. She wondered where he went off to so early then she turned to look at the necklace. Maybe she'd donate it to the church fair when she got home – someone might like it.

After taking a few sips of tea, Catherine placed her purse over her shoulder and left the cottage. She locked the door and looked around. It was a quiet, sleepy time, with lots of night people certainly still in bed.

In town, she tried to seem interested in what each shop had to offer, always observant, yet she knew that she would buy the muffins and coffee where she always did – food was dependably good there. She bought a loaf of day-old bread, two cranberry orange muffins, two coffees and two sugar cookies. She reasoned that with kite flying they might need some extra energy.

Back at her cottage, Catherine slipped into her car and drove to the rocky length of shore. Luke's car was there; he was positioned on their rock. It felt reliable, this time with him.

"Hey," she hollered to him, "are you ready to have your bat get beaten?"

Luke turned around and smiled as he saw her approaching him. He stood, took the bakery bag from her and then offered his hand to help her balance and then sit on the rock. He sat down next to her, handing her the bag. Catherine reached in for the bread and Luke took the tie from the wrapper. They tossed chunks of bread to the gulls who now waited each morning for their treats.

Catherine took the muffins and coffee from the bag and, with a little smile, told Luke they also had cookies.

"Are the cookies your consolation prize for losing at kite flying?" he asked.

"For that remark," she said, "I may eat *both* of the cookies."

They took their time enjoying the sea, the gulls, the food and one another. After a little more than an hour, they agreed to try out their new treasures. On the grass by their cars, they secured their strings to the decorative kites and held them high as they let them go to Catherine's squeals of laughter. Luke's kite soared, dipped and fell. He retrieved it as Catherine's kite obeyed the rules of the sky. Then he tried again. This time, the bat lifted, circled, and soared higher than Catherine's red dragon. She had not recalled ever having this much fun, running, watching, pulling and releasing. At one point, their strings became entangled and the kites bumped into each other then crashed to thick grass. Catherine laughed so hard she fell to the ground – Luke laughed and tried to loosen his kite before Catherine could manage the same. When she noted his endeavor to win, Catherine scrambled to her feet, untangled the kites, and then took off running. A few observers watched them, laughing at their antics.

By the time they had flown the kites for more than an hour, they were exhausted and happily pulled them down, winding up the string. They leaned against Luke's car and laughed, Catherine brushing her hair back from her face, Luke brushing grass and bits of sand from his clothes.

"That was a good workout," he said.

"Fire Dragon won," Catherine said.

"I beg your pardon," Luke replied. "Blood Bat did

95

miraculously up there."

"Oh, there you go," Catherine teased, "using your priestly powers to invoke a miracle."

Luke gave her a sleek smile that caused the side of his nice mouth to twist. "Oh, I think Super Bat did well enough not to depend on a miracle."

Catherine laughed. "It was fun; we should do this again soon."

"I need a cookie," Luke sulked.

Catherine laughed as she opened her car door, deposited her kite and reached for the cookies. She gave one to Luke and took a bite from the other. They mumbled between swallows that the treats were good.

"I love cookies," Luke said. "I like to make them, too. They make the whole house smell good."

Catherine laughed. "You bake cookies?"

"Hey," he said, "some of the best cooks in the world are men. However, I'm not fussy about who makes them as long as I get to devour them."

Catherine smiled and nodded.

"What did you do with that necklace?" he asked.

"Nothing, it's where we left it. When I get around to going back home, maybe I'll donate it to the church fair. I wish I knew where it came from."

When they were leaving the rocky shoreline at three, Luke asked about later. "It's Saturday – tonight in town could be jumping; might be a good chance to spot Trini. Would you care for a walk and dinner?"

Catherine hesitated at her car. Was this relationship spinning out of control? She feared it could all end and she'd be left longing.

"Catherine? Later?"

She smiled as she climbed into the driver's seat and started the engine. "Sure," she said, "about eight again?"

Luke shoved his kite into the trunk of his car and said, "That's good, but can we eat first this time?" He patted his slim abdomen. "A guy could get hungry waiting until later."

Catherine smiled. "I'm fine with eating earlier. See you at eight."

She pulled away wondering what kind of idiot she was. She had always been fearful of feelings for someone who might not be emotionally available. Something about Luke compelled her to take a chance.

Back at the cottage, Catherine rifled through her sparse selection of clothing. What would she wear to dinner? She had an ankle length skirt she'd worn before with Luke; she'd wear it tonight with a deep purple blouse, blending in with the beach strip attire, free and easy.

As it was beginning to turn dark, Catherine looked over at the green cottage. It was quiet and there was no light from the windows, no car in the driveway. She hoped the girl was okay. As she began to turn away, she noticed movement behind the window, a shadowy figure wearing a white t-shirt beneath what seemed to be a gray cardigan. Only the left shoulder of the person was visible. One dainty palm pressed against the glass for just a moment then the figure moved away. Catherine stood and stared at the window for a few moments.

When Luke knocked gently at her door, Catherine opened it and watched his eyes travel over her from auburn hair to sandaled feet. "Nice color on you," he said indicating the purple top.

Catherine smiled and thanked him – all in black, he didn't look too shabby himself, but it did serve to remind her of his former vocation.

They walked in town among the crowd, ate dinner at a place specializing in seafood then walked for two additional hours. At the edge of town where they were closest to their cottages, Luke asked, "What do you think? It's nearly one. Do you want to continue?"

"My feet hurt," Catherine said. "I think I'm done for tonight."

They moved slowly back toward the cottages, each of them saying little, and when they did it was to comment on the soft breeze, the bright moon. When they reached Catherine's place, Luke took her hands for just a moment. She thought he might pull her to him, but he didn't. He waited until she unlocked the door and stepped inside, switching a light on, and then before he left he told her he hoped she'd have a good rest.

"Wait," Catherine called to him. "Are we meeting tomorrow?"

"I'll pick up some breakfast for us. See you at eleven," he said, and then he was gone.

Catherine closed her door and locked it. She lay down across her bed completely clothed, except for her shoes, and slept.

Chapter Seven

Sunday morning brought a cool breeze into Catherine's room and she could hear church bells in the distance. She had not seen a church in the center of town but knew that there must be a few denominations in the area. Without thinking why, church suddenly held appeal. There were good people there, people with good intentions. Although Catherine had not cared for organized religion, the sense of community at church was admirable. She thought about going then decided instead to make tea and say a few of her own little prayers. She was not too proud to beg on her sister's behalf.

Just before eleven, Catherine drove to the rocky shoreline where she felt elated to see Luke sitting in his car. As she parked and turned her engine off, he walked over to her with a white bakery bag in one hand.

"Good morning," he said as he opened her car door. "Did you sleep well?"

"Actually I did. I fell asleep across my bed rather than in the rocking chair. What did you bring for us in that bag? I've had tea, but that's it."

"Come on," he said extending a hand to her. "I'll show you when we get ourselves settled."

They walked across the street and down a few cement steps to the rocks and their chosen space

99

halfway to the rushing sea. The seagulls were nearby and flew closer, positioning themselves for Luke's offerings. He tossed several large slices of bread to them, handed Catherine the remaining loaf, then from the white bag he took two large cups of coffee, two small, clear plastic containers of mixed fruit, and last, two blueberry-walnut scones.

Catherine tossed bread to the gulls and then looked at the tempting food.

"This looks nice," she said. "Where did you get the fruit?"

"The bakery was out of day-old bread, so I went next door to a deli and managed to get bread as well as the fruit cups. I thought it wouldn't hurt either one of us to eat something healthy."

Catherine smiled. "You're right, and it looks great. I buy oranges in town, so I get a little nutrition, but I admit I'm a carb and coffee fiend."

They ate their fruit first then drank coffee with their scones. When they'd finished their breakfast, they sat with their coffee, content with their view and one another's company.

Catherine did not show her amusement, but she took note of the fact that every time they met on those rocks, Luke managed to edge a bit closer to her. She did not object. He was handsome, charming, intelligent, and just vulnerable enough to have a sweetness about him that she had not known in other men. She understood quite clearly, she was hooked.

After about fifteen minutes of not speaking, Luke turned to Catherine. "We should come down here some evening at sunset and see if we can figure out where these guys go. They're apparently elusive little creatures."

Catherine agreed. "I had a cat like that when I was younger. My parents and I kept her inside so that she wouldn't harm the birds and chipmunks but at times she'd hide on us as we were going to bed. We'd search high and low, thinking that somehow she'd snuck outside, then after a thorough search and no clue where she was, out she'd strut like she was proud to have had one up on us lowly humans."

Luke laughed. "No pets now?"

"Not yet. At the age of nineteen, she went to sleep one night and that was the end. The apartment I have now does not permit pets, but I want to move, so I'll find a place where I can have what I want."

"Another cat?"

"I like everything with four feet," she said, "but a cat is a strong contender."

Luke nodded. "I like animals, too. I had a dog and a cat as a kid. The pastor at the church where I was assigned had a dog. Sadly, I miss the dog more than the pastor."

Catherine laughed. "Was he grouchy?"

"No, the dog actually had a very even personality."

Catherine gave Luke an intolerant look and he laughed. "The pastor was okay, a little on the fire and brimstone side, but not really grouchy. I was wondering if you'd like to take a little break with me today. I thought we could go inland twenty miles and I could show you my former church and school. There are some nice little restaurants in the area where we could have an early dinner."

Catherine thought about the doubts she'd felt earlier in their relationship – that maybe he hadn't been a priest at all. She fervently hoped that her suspicions were wrong and that her instincts were right, that Luke was the man she wanted him to be.

"It sounds like a pleasant change," she said. "I'd like that."

When Luke arrived at her cottage later that day, Catherine was ready, wearing her black dress and sandals, her hair hanging loosely about her shoulders. His eyes appraised her from head to toe as she opened the car door before he could get out and open it for her.

"I like that dress a lot," he said.

Catherine knew and smiled as she buckled herself in. "Where are we off to?"

"Toward Providence. You'll see."

They were quiet for a few minutes when Luke asked about the necklace. "So, anything new about the jewelry left at your door?"

"Nothing. And the other strange thing is that I haven't seen anyone come or go from the cottage next door. Normally there are doors slamming, voices. I wonder if they were here on vacation and have gone - I kind of hope so; they were strange."

"How so?" Luke asked.

Catherine wrinkled her nose a bit and tried to explain. "I only saw the girl a couple of times. She looked emaciated. The fellow, who was pretty young, maybe in his early twenties, changed his clothes a lot. He'd go out in a blue shirt and come back in a tan jersey. It was as if he had another place he went and changed. He was also rough with the girl; I could hear

102

an angry tone to his voice. I hope they're gone."

"Do you suppose that necklace was meant for her, for the girl?" Luke asked.

Catherine shook her head. "I don't know. I suppose so. If they want it, they can have it. It's still on the coffee table where we left it."

Within a half hour, Luke pulled up to a stone church. "This is it," he said. "This is where I spent close to three years, and that building to the right is the school where I taught. I had a dual responsibility here, to assist the aging pastor and to teach math to seventh and eighth graders. It was a nice existence, but I wasn't being true to myself."

"And where you are now in Vermont, is that more who you are?"

Luke nodded. "Yes."

"It has no religious affiliation?"

"None."

Catherine's eyes scanned the area, the church and school all built of stone and stucco. The grounds were green and manicured – it was pretty, draped in red maples and one large weeping willow. She could envision Luke there in his black robes, the garment flowing in the gentle breeze. She thought about the couple, the woman and man who were both attracted to him. She could see why.

"There's a little restaurant just out of town I think you'd like. They have some great home cooking and the desserts are incredibly good and bad." He smiled as he looked at her, the auburn hair against the black dress, her blue eyes sparkling.

"By 'bad' I suppose you mean that the desserts are

103

tempting and high in calorie."

"Oh no," he said, "they're loaded up with broccoli and green beans – they just *taste* like they're bad for us."

Catherine looked out through her side window and smiled. Within minutes, they were at the restaurant. As they walked inside she thought about how soothing it was to know where Luke had served as a priest. If he'd been trying to hide an alternate profession, he wouldn't have taken her to his former church where she could easily check that he'd actually been there.

They were seated at a table near a window where they could see a small pond with koi and lush greenery. The place, inside and out, was calming.

Back at their cottages by dusk, Catherine thanked Luke for a wonderful outing and change of pace.

"Will you go into town tonight?" he asked.

Catherine hesitated. "I can't say I want to, but I feel this need to keep on top of this. Trini is here somewhere – I know she is. I need one little glimpse of her, one instant of knowing that she's okay. Yes, I'll go into town about ten and have a look around."

"I'll go with you," he said.

"You don't have to, Luke. I was doing this for a few weeks before I met you."

"I know," he said, "but I think it looks more natural for you to be with someone. I also think it's safer."

She smiled at him and briefly touched his arm before she got out of the car. "Okay," she said, "I'd love the company."

When Luke knocked at her door later, he had

changed into jeans and a t-shirt. Catherine had changed into jeans and a pale blouse. They were dressed for the strip, their clothing casual, similar to everyone else.

While they did not see anyone who even slightly resembled Trini, Catherine caught sight of the young fellow from the green cottage. He was leaning against a telephone poll talking to a young girl, and it was not the girl she had seen at the cottage. Now she was concerned – what had happened to that poor, frail girl? She pointed him out to Luke, relayed her fears, and then they walked on.

It was a Sunday night and by one in the morning, the crowd had thinned. Catherine and Luke decided that many of them probably had work the next day and had to end their partying a little earlier than usual. They walked back to their cottages and at Catherine's door said they'd see one another in the morning at the shoreline, and then stood awkwardly, not touching, before they said goodnight.

As Catherine stepped inside her cottage, she closed and locked the door, and then she pulled the lace aside and peered out through the small window. She watched as Luke inserted the key in his lock and stepped inside, closing the door behind him. She looked around at the dim and dismal room. Something had to give pretty soon – it was becoming unbearable. She thought about her life, how she'd believed in her long-term relationship and then he died. She thought about her childhood, a not-so-bad period of years she was content to leave alone. There had been nothing unusual to analyze – she'd had friends, dances, sleepovers, all the normal activities of a typical teen.

Catherine walked to the bedroom, looked at the darkened windows next door, then walked to the rocking chair in the front room and sat down. She rocked back and forth thinking about not losing herself by falling for Luke. She was there for a purpose and she needed to keep that in mind. Besides, in a matter of a few weeks, he would head back to his teaching position in Vermont, far removed from this coast and from her. If only she could find Trini.

Dozing in the chair, Catherine was wakened by the sound of a car door. She looked out to her driveway, then to the one next door. She watched as a shadowy figure moved about, and then with the aid of the streetlight, she could see that the figure was the young man who had been there before. He was walking around the outside of the cottage. He didn't open the front door; his gait reflected impatience, as if he was angry. Within moments, he was back in his car and gone.

Catherine stood at the bedroom window and wondered what that was all about. Had he forgotten something? She'd seen him in town – if he wasn't living next to her, where was he living? Where was the dark-haired girl? This place was beginning to get on her nerves. She sat down on the bed and then lay back thinking about her father. She wondered what Helga had been like. Was she a beautiful blonde like Trini? Catherine's mother had been stunning as a young woman – at sixty years of age, the woman was still attracting second looks and more men than she cared to know. She loved to read, she loved living with or near her sister in Arizona, and that was enough.

When the admission came from her father on his deathbed, Catherine recalled her mother's stoic reaction. The woman held her husband's hand, and when he drifted into a morphine-induced coma, she walked quietly out of the room, no tears. When he was gone, she told Catherine that somewhere out in the world, she had a sister named Trini Bauer.

Catherine took a few deep breaths thinking about that night less than a year ago. She decided almost immediately that she would try to locate her sibling. When the investigation began, the police department where she worked told her to leave it alone – the girl was trouble. For weeks into months, Catherine sought information from every available source. When her chief insisted she stop, Catherine quit the force. She recalled what it felt like to relinquish her badge. She knew then that she would never again be a police officer.

She raised herself to a sitting position on the bed, then stood and walked to the front room and the rocking chair. She glanced at the necklace surrounded by newsprint then closed her eyes against all the uncertainties. What in her life was positive? Luke, Luke was positive. She wanted to wrap her arms around his lanky form and never let go. She'd never felt that depth of emotion before – it both sustained and devoured her.

When Catherine opened her eyes to the morning light, sun drifted in past the lace curtain and rested on the glimmering necklace. She couldn't take her eyes from it, the way it seemed to have a life of its own. She reached forward and touched it, half expecting it to feel warm, even hot. Then she moved her left forefinger

107

over the stones. They glinted with light in such a way that she was certain it wasn't just her synesthesia – surely this necklace would enchant anyone.

Catherine carefully lifted the necklace so that it draped across her hands. She stood and walked to the bathroom mirror as she placed it around her neck, its V formation of blue and clear stones just below her throat. She touched the stones again, and as much as she knew this wasn't a piece she would ever wear, she admitted to herself that it had strength in its design and color. She unfastened the lock at the back of her neck and carried the jewelry back to its box where she placed it gently. The sun had moved and allowed the jewels to sleep.

Catherine showered and changed into fresh jeans and a dark green shirt, rolling the long sleeves back to just above her elbows. Close to eleven, she drove to the rocks where Luke was leaning against his car, waiting with coffee and treats from the bakery. He sauntered over to her and opened her door.

"Good morning," he said.

Catherine smiled at him. "Hi."

She slipped out of her car and stood, then gave her door a right hip closing; she kept in step with Luke as they headed for the rocks.

"When are we flying our kites again?" she asked. "Unless, of course, you're afraid my dragon will beat your bat again."

Luke looked at her and grinned. "Bring it on, Baby."

Catherine stopped and looked at him in astonishment. "What kind of talk is that from a priest?"

Luke faced her with a threatening look. "If you don't quit with the priest stuff..."

Catherine laughed. "Okay, but we should have a flying competition again soon."

From their rock, they tossed bread to the gulls and then sat down to have coffee and corn muffins laced with cranberries and pecans. Catherine took a bite and sighed with delight.

"These are so good," she said. "They remind me of the corn muffins my mother made at Thanksgiving. She cut tiny pieces of cranberry sauce into the muffins after she'd spooned the mixture into the baking cups. I'll have to make them sometime."

"Great idea," Luke said, "and you can invite me over."

Catherine shook her head. "Afraid not here - I have no oven in my cottage. Do you?"

Luke smiled. "No oven. But maybe you could invite me to your apartment sometime. Or you could use the oven in my Vermont kitchen."

Catherine finished the last of her muffin and swallowed some coffee. Was he really inviting her to visit with him in Vermont?

"My apartment is in Massachusetts. And where in Vermont are you teaching and living? I don't think you ever told me."

Luke looked at her. "I read maps – I can find my way to Massachusetts. But if you'd prefer Vermont, I'm about halfway across the state, past Woodstock, near Killington. It's beautiful."

"Do you like it better there than here by the sea?"

Luke pursed his lips and then looked at her again.

109

"It's a toss-up. I grew up near the ocean so it's important to me. But Vermont's hills are mesmerizing and peaceful. I'm surprised how much I feel at home there. And in a few hours, I can be right here on these rocks with these gulls."

Catherine smiled then looked out to the glimmering horizon.

"You know," he said, "I've come to terms with the question about where seagulls sleep. I've decided that they're smart. Wherever they go, they're hunkered down and safe, and that's what's important. Maybe it isn't ours to know. It may be best for them that we *don't* know."

Catherine thought about what he said. He'd given the subject consideration and she liked that about him.

"To me," he said, "life is a circle. We're all connected: humans, animals, trees, flowers, bumblebees. We need one another."

Catherine looked down at her sandaled feet and then squinted as she gazed out to sea. He was right, she agreed with him completely, but she didn't say a word. What she thought of next was seeing him in Vermont where she'd bake him cranberry corn muffins and anything else he wanted. Maybe it was a far-reaching dream, but she decided to hang on to it for now – it was deliciously inviting to consider.

Catherine would have liked to ask him more about the priesthood, his beliefs, his hopes. She decided not to push it. Being at his side, sharing simple meals, walking the beach strip late at night, feeding the gulls, were important in revealing his character. She liked everything about him, perhaps too much.

When the afternoon became gray and clouds threatened rain, Luke suggested they get to their cars and go back to the cottages.

"What will you do tonight if it's raining?" he asked in the parking lot. "You wouldn't go into town, would you? I doubt many would be out in a storm."

Catherine slipped in behind the steering wheel and started her engine, Luke by her window. "I guess I'll have to see what happens. This might be just the kind of night that Trini would feel safe going out. She could hide beneath an umbrella or conceal her face wearing a rain jacket with a hood. I don't know what I'll do. It hasn't rained since I arrived here."

"If you go, I'll go with you," he said. "We can share my black, priestly umbrella."

Catherine smiled. "I'm not saying a word."

Luke went to his car and Catherine pulled away smiling. This time, it was Luke making comments about having been a priest and, proudly, she had managed to keep her tongue in her mouth.

With a dark night came pouring rain and streaks of lightning. Catherine sat in her rocking chair with a book and a dim light. When she heard a knock at the door, it startled her. She looked out through the window and saw that it was Luke, standing there with a jacket over his head. She opened the door and stepped aside as he walked in.

"That's nasty out there," he said. "I hope you've decided to stay in tonight."

Catherine offered him a towel, which he declined. She offered him hot tea, which he accepted.

"I think lightning changed the course of my plans,"

111

she said on her way to the kitchen.

She returned a few minutes later with two mugs of tea. They sat, he on the sofa, she in her chair. Luke leaned forward and picked up the necklace.

"It's distinctive, isn't it? I really have to wonder which of your admirers left this for you," he teased.

Catherine lifted her mug of tea and blew on it before taking a sip. It was too hot to drink, but she held it anyway.

"I actually tried it on," she said. "It's pretty, but I like simple jewelry, chains with pendants. This looks like something royalty would wear. I'd love to know where it came from."

"Have you thought about taking it to the police in case someone is looking for it?"

Catherine shrugged. "That's not a bad idea. It could have some sentimental value to someone."

Luke settled the necklace back into the newsprint and box in which it arrived. He picked up his tea, took a few swallows then sat back on the sofa, crossing his right leg over his left knee.

"You know," he said, "these cottages aren't half bad if you have someone to share them with."

Catherine smiled at his sweetness. He was right – being with someone you cared for changed the prospective.

"Are you tired?" he asked. "I can leave; I didn't mean to intrude. Looks like you have a book for company."

"I brought several books with me," she said. "I haven't read even one. I've been so distracted by this search for my sister. I started this; it's a biography of

Mary Lincoln."

"Sounds interesting. Is that your preference for reading material, non-fiction?"

"No, I read everything; I can get lost in a good novel. What about you?"

Luke picked up Catherine's book and turned it over to read the back. "I read a variety of things, too – I enjoy a good mystery."

"Do you play card games?" Catherine asked as they sipped tea.

"Old-Maid and Fish as a kid, a little Poker in college. Did you have something in mind? Do we have cards?"

Catherine stood and walked to a small drawer in an otherwise empty chest. From there she extracted a deck of well-worn cards and held them out for Luke to see.

"Fish or Poker?" she asked with a smile as she playfully spilled the cards onto the coffee table.

Luke organized the disarrayed deck and smiled. "Fish."

Until nearly two in the morning, they played and laughed, talking easily with one another against claps of thunder and streaks of neon lightning. In a subsiding storm, Luke donned his light jacket and went to his own cottage.

Chapter Eight

At ten in the morning, Catherine slipped into her car and drove to the town's police station with the boxed necklace next to her in the seat. She pulled into the parking lot and hesitated. She looked at the gems one more time – the necklace was pretty but coupled with the fact that it was not her style, the jewelry did not belong to her. Someone would probably be glad to have it back.

She walked into the small police station and was met by a female clerk. Catherine explained that the box had arrived on her doorstep, but she was certain not to be the intended recipient. The clerk asked Catherine to fill out a form with basic contact information and thanked her for bringing the necklace in. She gave Catherine a receipt for the item, which Catherine thought was a good idea. She wasn't so sure that her former police department would have made that gesture.

With one last glance to the necklace, Catherine smiled at the clerk, took her receipt, and walked out to her car. She drove into town, stopped at the bakery for muffins, gull bread, and coffee. It was just after eleven when she arrived at the shoreline where Luke waited, leaning against his car.

They walked in sync together across the rocks and

sat in their claimed space. The gulls were waiting as if they wore watches.

Luke unfastened the bread loaf's end and sailed slices through the air like Frisbees. Catherine laughed at the graceful show the birds performed, soaring and dipping to catch their expected food.

She sat down and proceeded to take the muffins from the white bag, then the coffee. Having doled out the remaining bread, Luke joined her, anxious for a sip of his hot brew.

"Oh, that's good," he said as he placed the large cup on a flat area of rock and reached for a muffin. "What's the flavor of the day?" he asked as he lifted a light brown treat to his mouth."

Catherine looked at him and smiled. "Pumpkin spice." She took a bite and sighed, "This is delicious, but it does remind me that fall is coming."

"Is that a bad thing?" he asked as he patted his lips with a napkin.

Catherine wore a sad expression. "Autumn is my favorite time of year. I cherish the approaching holidays, but this summer has been stressful. I shouldn't feel attachment to this place, but I do. I need so much to locate Trini and I can't stay here forever. They drain the water from these cottages in October and close them up. And I'll miss this, breakfast on the rocks with the seagulls."

Luke gave her a serious but teasing look. "I didn't hear a thing about me in that statement."

Catherine smiled but she nearly cried. How was she going to face each morning without Luke?

"I took the necklace to the police," she said.

115

Luke nodded his approval. "I think that was a good idea. What are we up to today?"

"We?" Catherine asked.

"Well," he began, "now that my aunt has left for North Carolina, I have absolutely nothing to do. I thought I might follow you around."

Catherine laughed. "I'm sure that's because I lead such an exciting life. If you're willing to roam the town streets with me tonight, I might let you win at Fish."

Luke permitted part of a smile to grace his lips as he kept his eyes to the sea.

"I think we may need to rename that game Pure Shark."

Catherine laughed. She liked games and she liked to win.

They spent almost two hours on the rocks, watching the sea wrestle with the shore, seeming to struggle with the decision to stay or leave. Catherine and Luke packed up their breakfast trash and reluctantly left the area. She decided to canvas the shops for new sandals and maybe a new blouse or two. She hadn't thought that she would meet anyone for whom she would develop an interest – a wardrobe had been the last thing on her mind.

Luke mentioned that he was hitting a laundromat and picking up a few groceries. "I should make you dinner," he said as they were approaching their cars.

"You cook?"

"Not really, but what can you do to spaghetti and salad?"

Catherine laughed. "We could order pizza."

"Thanks for having faith in me," he said.

116

"There you go with that priest lingo again," she teased.

"Okay, so we'll order pizza. Would you like to come to my cottage, or do we just want to have pizza out in town?"

Catherine's expression became serious. "Good thought. We could have pizza out. That's the kind of food young people favor; maybe we'll have some luck seeing Trini. Wouldn't that be wonderful? I want it so much."

They agreed to meet in the street at eight that evening. They'd walk to town for beer and pizza, keeping their eyes open.

While the evening was softened by Luke's company, Catherine found herself feeling edgy, always on alert for a glimpse of her sister, or someone who might add the smallest piece of information to the girl's whereabouts. They walked; they ate and observed; they walked again until after midnight. It was mentally and physically exhausting.

At her door, after saying goodnight, Catherine started to insert her key in the lock; she turned and called softly to Luke who was halfway across the street to his own cottage.

He returned to her side and she whispered, "My door was unlocked. I think someone broke in."

Luke looked at the door's handle; it had been tampered with.

"Come over to my place," he said. "We need to call the police."

Catherine hesitated. "If you stay here, outside, I could go in and see if anything looks disturbed."

"Catherine," Luke said with a low but determined voice, "you can't do that. There could be someone inside with a weapon. We're calling the police." He took her hand and urged her across the street where he made the call on his cell phone. Within minutes, a cruiser arrived.

Catherine and Luke walked across to two police officers and introduced themselves quietly. With a gun drawn, one officer opened the door while the other followed. Having instructed Catherine and Luke to stay back, they entered the house and within less than ten minutes, they were back out.

"You definitely had company," the first officer told Catherine. "Anyone you know who might have been after something in particular?"

"No," Catherine said. "Can I go in?"

The officers held the door ajar for her as she and Luke stepped inside. A small table was on its side. Clothing in the bedroom was askew. The kitchen cupboards were open and the two pans in the place were on the floor.

Catherine looked around. As a former officer, she'd seen this sort of thing before.

"We'll file a report," the first officer said. "I'll need some information from you," he told Catherine. They sat down in the front room, Luke by Catherine's side on the sofa. With nothing missing, the incident was reported as a break-in rather than a theft.

As they were leaving, the officers assured Catherine that they would keep a patrol car on alert in her area. She should be vigilant and she should report anyone suspicious in the vicinity.

When they had gone, Luke placed his large hand over one of Catherine's. "Are you okay?"

Catherine nodded. "Yes, just a little shaken. It's such an invasion of privacy to think of someone being here, going through my belongings. I filed so many of these reports when I was on the force, but I never understood the emotional trauma."

They sat quietly for a few minutes before Luke suggested they go to his place and have some tea.

"I want to stay here and put things back in order," she said. "But thank you."

"Then I'm staying, too," he said. "I'll make us some tea – you put your things where they belong. Maybe we can get a little rest once we calm down. This is ridiculous. I really have a hard time with anyone thinking it's okay to break into someone's property. Do you ever get over that, even as a police officer?"

Catherine shook her head. "Maybe after years on the force, but no, I was amazed at the attitude of thieves, that what was yours was theirs. I'm not sure I'd ever *want* to get used to it – it's plain wrong."

They spent the next two hours drinking tea as Catherine folded clothes and Luke washed pans and utensils that had been left in disarray. He straightened her cupboards and walked around the small place, looking for anything out of order. At one point, he stopped at the small front window and pulled the lace curtain aside just enough to see that the view to his cottage was direct.

"You must be tired," Catherine said to Luke as she sat in her rocking chair and he sat on the sofa. "Why don't you go home and get some rest?"

119

"I'll rest where you rest," he said. "If you want to stay here, I'll stay here as well. If you want to come over to my place, that works too."

Catherine closed her eyes. "I'll stay here. Stretch out on the sofa if you'd like. There are blankets on the shelf in the closet."

"I'm fine," he said, and they both closed their eyes before sunlight filtered in and around the room as if touching and healing injured objects. Catherine rested but did not sleep. Luke did the same, every little while opening his eyes to observe her saddened face. She had turned in the rocker, her knees drawn up toward her chest, her face toward the window and door.

"Do you think they were after drugs?" Luke asked as they had morning tea.

"Maybe, or items to sell for drugs. I brought nothing of value with me; I must have been a disappointment. I keep my laptop in the car – thankfully, they didn't break into that. I suppose it would have been too conspicuous."

Luke looked at her with compassion and Catherine caught his glance.

"We should plan to meet on the rocks at eleven," she said. "I think I'll take a shower and change. Maybe you'd like to go home and do the same."

At any other time Luke might have thought she was trying to get rid of him, but what he understood was that Catherine needed the restoring sea – their routine of having breakfast on the rocks with the gulls was reassuring and soothing.

"Are you sure you'll be all right? I can stay while you shower."

"I'm okay," she said.

Luke took his tea mug to the kitchen sink and then walked to the front door. "I'll pick up the coffee, bread and muffins this morning. See you at eleven."

When he had gone, Catherine locked her door and stared down at the handle. It was tainted, touched by an invasive stranger. She walked to the kitchen and soaked paper towels with dish detergent and water, returning to the front door which she scrubbed inside and out. She took a hot shower and changed into jeans and a navy blue shirt. She brushed her freshly washed hair and, with it still damp, went to meet Luke on the rocks.

Standing at the shore, she could see him sitting in their usual place and she stopped. She thought about what she was going to do when he returned to Vermont. How was she going to cope in his absence? This was a man and a relationship for which she had no explanation. He had made his mark on her soul and she wished she understood why. No one else had ever made her feel this way before. She could not reason enough to wish she'd never met him – he was worth knowing if only briefly, but it was going to destroy something inside of her to lose him – she knew this for certain.

As she watched him, he turned around, almost as if he'd sensed her being there.

"Hey," he called and waved. "The gulls are waiting."

Catherine smiled and watched her step as she moved toward him and then sat down. Luke placed a cup of coffee in her hands and announced that they had egg and cheese on croissants for breakfast.

"Wow," she said. "What's the occasion?"

121

Luke looked at her and smiled.

"Nourishment; I thought you needed some protein after last night."

Catherine reached into the bag and placed one sandwich in Luke's hands. She held the other wrapped sandwich in her lap as she untied the bread for the gulls. Luke took about half of the loaf and began breaking the pieces in half, tossing them high in the air for the birds to glide toward and grasp in their sharp beaks. Catherine tossed the other half of the loaf and then they ate their own food, sipping their coffee as they gazed out to the rolling waves.

Luke looked at her. "I like your hair that way."

Catherine smiled. "Freshly washed? That's all I did with it other than a few strokes with a brush."

"I like it," he repeated. Catherine's auburn colored hair appeared dark red in the shimmering light of mid-day.

She sat quietly sipping her coffee almost afraid to say anything more. She was upset by the unsuccessful search for Trini, the break-in at her cottage, and the thought of losing Luke. What was she going to do without him? He had left an unyielding impression on her life. She questioned why her father's death, her mother's leaving for Arizona, or Riley's death from brain cancer, had not impacted her to this depth. Luke had serenely captured her heart, managing to bind it to his own.

Catherine's thoughts always returned to Trini. She needed to find her, but in doing so perhaps she could find herself. Having a sister who was an unknown, and who was missing, was unimaginable. Having her cottage broken into did not phase Catherine as much as it might have somewhere else; the drug scene at the beach was so rampant, it almost seemed like part of the package to have your place invaded.

"I'll miss this," Luke said, which startled Catherine.

He looked at her and saw no response.

"I'll miss our rock, our gulls. And I'll still wonder where they sleep," he said as he stretched his long legs before him and rested his eyes on the rolling green sea.

Catherine was silent. The lump in her throat almost prevented her from breathing.

"I'll miss *us,*" he said.

At that point Catherine closed her eyes and felt the traitorous tears stream from her eyes. Within moments, she felt Luke's hand at the back of her neck; he pulled her to him, kissing her as no one ever had. As they both moaned with the need for air, they lay back against the warm rocks where Catherine rested her head against his chest and draped her arm across his waist.

They stayed there, their eyes closed against the mid-day sun, content with one another's nearness. As gulls screeched above them, they each opened their eyes and squinted against the glare, then Luke sat up, gently pulling Catherine up to join him. He took his arm from around her shoulders and she wondered if he had second thoughts about touching her, kissing her. She wanted his nearness, something to dispel the impending departure for his return to Vermont.

After several silent moments, Catherine asked, "Do you ever think about that couple who had the interest in you?"

123

"Wow, where did that come from?" Luke asked as he looked into her blue eyes.

Catherine shrugged. "I just wondered how that affected your decision to leave the vocation of your choice."

Luke's lips pursed a bit as he thought and drew his eyes to the sea, then back at Catherine. "They had nothing to do with my departure. I'll admit the knowledge that they both seemed to have agendas was uncomfortable, but it wasn't a decision made based on anything but me. I didn't feel up to the task."

"Do you ever wonder if they're like the seagulls, sleeping where no one knows?"

Luke seemed thoughtful as he looked toward the sky and then the sea. "I suppose that's a possibility. My experience has been, and mind you I've always been well aware that a priest might not be the best source for marriage advice, that many people seem to hide in marriages for varying reasons. For some it's the commitment to family, for others it may be about financial security. It's complicated, and not always laced with love."

Catherine thought about what Luke said. He made sense.

"What are you going to do, Catherine? I'm worried about you living in the cottage after the break-in, and then there's that guy in town who accosted you. You can't think of staying here."

Catherine shook her head. "I have to. Where would I go, Luke? I have an apartment I should give up and no job. I should probably move near here and get something to do, even if it's work as a store clerk or a waitress. I can't abandon my search for Trini."

"I don't like it," he said.

"Got any ideas?" she asked, believing that question would close the topic.

"Yes, come with me."

Catherine took her eyes from Luke and stared at the sea. What was he thinking? As appealing as the thought was, being with Luke in the hills of Vermont, how could he imagine that she could relinquish this quest?

Before she could speak, Luke reached over and squeezed her hand. "Look, I know you're not giving up on finding your sister, but I'm concerned. It's going to be beyond difficult for me to leave here knowing what you're facing on a daily basis; those grueling walks in town, constantly searching, wondering where she is and how she is. I've thought about how I'd feel if it was *my* sister, and, of course, I *know* my sister. I wouldn't be able to give up the search either. Finding Trini is important to you, I know that, but not knowing her, not having a feeling for what she prefers to do, even to eat, makes it challenging."

Catherine nodded; she understood, but she had no choice when it came to her very personal search. The girl was a little island, and Catherine wasn't so far removed from that image herself.

"When will you leave?" she asked, afraid of the answer.

"In less than two weeks. I need to be back for student orientation."

Catherine swallowed back tears. It was going to be intolerable.

"Other than searching for your sister, which I am more than willing to do, I'd like us each to think of something special we could plan for – some little excursion, a get-a-way. Are you game?"

Catherine smiled and nodded, but she wondered how she'd get through what should be a joyous time with Luke when she would be thinking about how it might be the last time she would ever see him.

"I don't want to give you false hope, but I spoke with Charlie last night, my friend at school who told me about Trini's mother going back to Germany pregnant. He said he might have something more; he'll fill me in when I get back to school."

Catherine looked at Luke. "Couldn't he tell you now?"

"I caught him at a bad time; he was rushing out to catch a plane to the West Coast for two weeks. I promise, Catherine, if it's anything significant, I'll let you know."

Chapter Nine

Over the next few days, Catherine felt compelled to check on the cottage next door. She wondered if the occupants had gone. Almost overnight, they had disappeared. While Catherine had never spoken to either of them, there was a sense of loss she couldn't explain, seeing those windows darkened both day and night. The season, she supposed, was like that. People going back to their normal lives: summer ending, relationships disintegrating. She thought about Luke. Is that what they had, a summer interlude?

Catherine watched. She walked; she questioned shop owners and people she spoke to casually while having a sandwich or a cold drink. The routine only changed because of who she encountered. Someone had to know more about Trini, someone who was willing to part with the information.

Every day at eleven when she met Luke for breakfast on the rocks with the gulls, she thought about what he said: the question about where the sea birds found rest. That he would consider that, that he would care, impressed her. To find someone who thought about a winged creature when some considered them a nuisance was, to Catherine, admirable – heartwarming.

One week before his departure, after feeding the gulls and taking a few swallows of his morning coffee,

Luke looked at Catherine. "Where would you like to go? We need a day away, someplace where we can relax and have some fun; any ideas?"

Catherine took a deep breath and hoped he hadn't noticed. She shook her head and the wind pulled at her long hair, tossing auburn strands across her lips, as if to keep them still.

"Tell me what you like to do," he said. "We're already at the sea, so we don't want a place with water. There's a good zoo not far away, any interest? Shoot some ideas at me."

Catherine held on tightly to her coffee cup. "I'm not sure we should go anywhere, Luke. I could miss seeing Trini that one time."

Luke was silent for a moment as his dark eyes scanned the horizon. "Catherine, you need a little break. If your sister came out that one time, she'll appear another time. Come on, come and play with me for a day. I'm up for anything. Just name it."

Catherine sat for a few moments thinking and watching the surf thoroughly wash the rocks below. She looked at Luke and smiled. "I want to go to that huge mall in the city, the one with several levels. I want to spend some money, maybe I'll buy a reckless dress or an incredibly high-heeled pair of shoes. I feel like doing something completely nonsensical."

"I'll agree to that suggestion on one condition."

"What's that?" she asked.

"That you'll wear that reckless dress and those high-heeled shoes for *me*."

Catherine looked at him and laughed.

"And if you make one single remark about that not

being a priestly comment, I might have to get rough with you."

"Really?" she said with flirty eyes.

"You're incorrigible," he said. "Tomorrow we'll have a day at your majestic mall."

That night they walked the beach town's streets again and kept alert to anything new. What they found were less people. With August's end, many had moved on. In some ways, it made the search easier, but then Catherine began to wonder if that alone would cause Trini to conceal herself more. She had gone into hiding – the sparse population could put her in greater danger of being located by the two men in search of her. There didn't seem to be a scenario that worked in Catherine's favor.

When it was near midnight and Luke had walked Catherine to her door, he went into the cottage with her as he had since the break-in. He walked to the back door, to the windows, then back to the front door. Determining that everything was in order, he placed each of his large hands at the sides of her face and drew her to him. With one thorough kiss, he dropped his hands to her neck and then to her shoulders.

Catherine moved back just enough to suggest that he stop. He smiled and reached for the door handle. "We'll have breakfast at your mall tomorrow. I'll pick you up around nine and then we'll be on our way. I'll see you in the morning."

Catherine stared at the door when he left, then she locked it and sat in her rocking chair. She wondered why she'd been hesitant with him. Why did she back away?

129

She knew. She loved everything about this man, but thoughts of him leaving in little more than a week were torture. To some extent, moving away from him was proof to herself that she could let him go. It was a test.

The next day, Catherine heard Luke's car as he pulled up in front of her cottage at nine sharp. Dressed in tan slacks and a sheer navy blue shirt, she walked outside, locked her door then slid into the car with Luke.

His look was appreciative as his eyes traveled from her sandaled feet to her gleaming hair. "I took bread to the gulls," he said. "You're going to have to do that once I'm gone, you know."

Catherine's smile faded and she looked away from him.

"Hey, I'm just kidding," he said as he noticed her expression change. "I feel guilty eating in front of them, but those guys are pretty fair fishermen. They'll be fine without our flimsy carbohydrates."

Catherine stayed silent, not sure that she could speak. She didn't want to think about him leaving. And, in fact, she wasn't sure that she could go to those rocks ever again without Luke at her side.

Luke understood that his teasing hadn't gone over well. He stayed silent until they were near the city and could see the looming building where the mall was built over a picturesque river. "See?" he said. "Wishes do come true."

Catherine's eyes scanned the massive structure and she felt exhilaration for being there. Surely this was a place where people were happy, back-to-school shopping for their kids and themselves, finding a new outfit for fall.

Luke parked in a garage near the mall's entrance and turned off the engine.

"Are you hungry?" he asked. "There's a cafeteria in there, and if that's not your choice, there are probably a dozen little places where we can eat. What do you think?"

Catherine gathered her purse to her shoulder as she opened the car door. Luke walked around to her side, offering his hand as she stepped out of the vehicle. "I like the idea of the cafeteria," she said. "I don't know what I want; I'll be able to look at what they have. Are you okay with that?"

"I'm ready to eat a chair," he said. "The cafeteria sounds great."

As they walked in through rotating doors, Luke casually took Catherine's left hand in his right hand, guiding her to the elevator.

"It seems you know your way around here pretty well," she said when they stepped into the glass vehicle which rapidly moved them to the third floor.

Luke nodded. "I came here once in a while when I was one of those guys dressed in black."

Catherine smiled.

At their level, they walked less than thirty steps to the cafeteria and selected a table with a perfect view of the river below. The pink and white flowers dotting the river's curved edge made it look cared for and welcoming. They watched as people strolled along on the wide sidewalks or sat on ornate wrought iron benches.

"I'd love to go down there later," she said.

"We'll do it," Luke said. "After shopping for a bit, maybe we could grab a coffee and enjoy it by the water."

From the cafeteria, Catherine chose a small bowl of assorted melon chunks and a tomato and cheese omelet with tea. Luke chose a Mexican omelet with rye toast and black coffee.

As they ate, they watched the activity below; the pigeons walking on the sidewalks looked the size of sparrows from the cafeteria's height. Luke fetched them each a second cup of tea and coffee, then they walked the mall's wide aisles where Catherine browsed at fashions she would never wear. In one shop, she spotted a red dress. It had large white flowers as its print and, while it was sleeveless, she thought how nice it would be with a white sweater or a white blazer. She tried it on, bought it, then searched and found red shoes.

"I hope I'm going to see you in that dress," he said. "Let's do Ricardo's the night before I leave."

Catherine didn't know if she wanted to cry or beat him with her package. How could he be so insensitive? Did the man have no clue as to her feelings?

She decided to ignore his remark and did not give him a reply. She continued to shop. At a store window where a sofa was featured draped with an off-white throw and two attractive pillows, she stopped to look.

"Furniture?" he questioned.

"Just considering," she said. "My apartment is filled with hand-me-downs and, besides, I'm leaving there shortly. I'll need some new things eventually. I like the colors in this arrangement – the tan sofa, the

132

copper-toned pillows, neutral throw. That's my kind of furniture and accessories."

Luke smiled. "My, have we an interior designer little homebody here?"

Catherine stopped walking and looked at him. "Are all men oblivious to color schemes? Do all of you prefer big, bulky recliners even if they're an ugly orange with metallic gold polka dots?"

"Whew," he said as he urged her to walk. "I guess that put me in my place."

Catherine looked away from him and then walked to a jewelry store window. She looked at the rings, the bracelets, the earrings and necklaces.

"Anything there you particularly like?"

Catherine shook her head. "I just like to look. Some of it with the deep blue stones reminds me of that necklace, the one I left with the police. I wonder if anyone has claimed it."

"You could check," he suggested.

Catherine decided to change the subject. "What about *you* doing some shopping? Wouldn't you like a nice new shirt or sweater for going back to teach?"

"Sure," he said. "Help me choose something."

They walked into a men's shop and Catherine immediately walked to a mannequin with a beige shirt, striped brown tie and a coffee-with-cream colored V-neck sweater. "This," she said, "suits you."

"Okay. Select one more set for me."

Catherine looked at him and smiled. "Really? You agree with my taste?"

"Absolutely," he said.

Catherine transferred her shopping bag to Luke

133

and walked to a counter filled with sweaters in every color. She found one in a blue-green, and then a tie and shirt to match.

"These remind me of our ocean," he said.

"Exactly," she replied as she took back her package while he paid for his purchases.

"Are we ready for another coffee?" he asked two hours after breakfast.

"By the river?"

"Sure. After that, we can come back up here or move on. The day belongs to us, we're free as birds."

Sitting by the river, Catherine sipped hot coffee and looked pensive.

"Everything okay?" Luke asked noting her silence.

"Yes, I'm loving this. Thank you, Luke, I did need to get away. However, I have this thought in mind and you might think it's silly."

"Tell me about it," he urged.

"I'd like to go back into the mall. It's cheerful there, and I wouldn't mind finding a practical shirt to add to my present wardrobe. But most of all, I'd like to look for something pretty and youthful for Trini. I'm going to find her and I want a gift ready. I think I want to buy her something red, like my dress. Maybe a pretty blouse, or even a lightweight sweater. I just know I want it to be red."

Luke reached over and patted her hand as they sat on the bench by the river, then he folded his hand around hers as they sipped their coffee and watched the pigeons waddling along the edge of the very green grass.

After more than an hour, they left their packages in

Luke's car and went back into the mall. Catherine saw a red button-down sweater with tiny white flowers embroidered at the neck; it reminded her of the dress she'd purchased for herself, red with white flowers. She bought it for her sister.

Their purchases after that consisted of a pound of penuche for Luke's sweet tooth and a hand lotion with an almond aroma for Catherine. They sat in the cafeteria for one more coffee and a shared piece of cheesecake. Catherine applied some of the lotion to her hands. Luke watched her meticulously reaching between her fingers and smiled. "That stuff smells good enough to eat," he said.

"I love almond everything," she said.

"I'll remember that," he replied.

They were quiet for a few minutes, again with their eyes on the river below, the sun turning parts of the water to liquid gold.

"What's the most sensual part of the human form?" he asked out of the blue.

Catherine laughed. "You know, you're kind of a crazy guy to have been in your former profession."

Luke gave her a stern look.

"I didn't say a thing," she said. "Did I say the six-letter word?"

"So, answer my question," he said.

Catherine squirmed and thought about it. "I guess the eyes."

Luke shook his head from side to side. "I think it's the hands."

"I'm not sure I'm going there," she said with a smile.

Virginia Young

Luke leaned forward just a bit, setting his coffee cup down on the small, circular table.

"Look," he said as he splayed his hands and fingers on the table. "Our hands do so much. They feed us, they bathe us, they bandage us when we're injured, they button and unbutton our clothing, they groom our hair, pull on our socks, tie our shoes, prepare our food, they stroke our pets, they wash our dishes, they touch those we love. It's endless. I think the most sensual part of us is our hands."

Catherine stared into his chocolate brown eyes. "I agree," she said, and then they were quiet as they observed the river below and drank their coffee.

The ride back toward their beach cottages took forty minutes. They chatted amiably about the plush scenery along the way, traffic, and the varying shapes and sizes of houses in diversified New England.

"I've always thought that the people in this part of the country were like their homes, not afraid to be different. I wouldn't want to live anywhere else but New England," Catherine said.

"Have you been to Vermont?" Luke asked glancing over at her while they stopped at a red light.

"I've been all over New England," she said. "My parents took summer vacations at places along the coast of Maine, the hills of Vermont and New Hampshire, and day trips to the lower three of the six states. I love it all. I've been to the Midwest and to the West Coast. It's all nice but, still, New England is best. What about you? What is your choice?"

Luke kept his eyes to the road as he drove. "I went to school in LA for a few years before the seminary,

136

and I visited New Mexico and Arizona. They're great places, all of them, but New England is home."

Catherine rested her head against the back of the seat and looked out through the window on her side. They both loved New England, but did their homes have to be so far apart? She could easily see Luke in Vermont's rugged terrain, cross-country skiing with those lanky legs, or gliding across the ice on a frozen pond. She could also visualize him on the beach, simply sitting and enjoying the sprawling rocks by the sea.

"We'll be back at the beach in about ten minutes," Luke said after a length of silence. "How do you feel about dinner?"

"Oh, not yet," she said patting her stomach. "But you've given me such a wonderful day, how about if I treat you to dinner in a couple of hours? Would you be okay with that timing?"

"Sure, but I'm not sure I want dinner. I could go for some appetizers and wine."

Catherine nodded. "Let's do the appetizer then; that sounds good to me. Maybe around eight?"

Luke slowly threaded his way through the beach strip, maneuvering the car around pedestrians oblivious to traffic. He pulled the car up to Catherine's front door and stopped. "Eight o'clock sounds great. Where would you like to go?"

"Would you mind if we stayed in town? The Shell Café is kind of nice, not the typical little beach place, but still, it might be something that would hold appeal to someone like Trini."

"That's fine," he said. "We'll walk then." He started to get out of the car to see Catherine inside.

She reassured him that it was daylight; he need not worry, she'd be fine.

"I'll see you about eight then," he said.

Catherine unlocked the door and walked into the cottage. Everything was as she had left it. She decided to take a quick shower and then make phone calls to her mother and a friend. She would relax for a little while, perhaps read one of her novels. It had been a wonderful day with Luke – his patience as she browsed the dresses and shoes, and his good humor, made shopping a pleasure. He was an amazing find.

At precisely eight o'clock, Luke was knocking on Catherine's door. She opened it to see him totally in black. She smiled, invited him in, but said nothing of his attire. She was wearing chino pants and a pale pink long-sleeved jersey. It would be a casual night at the Shell Café.

"Let me just grab my purse from the bedroom," she said.

When she returned, Luke opened the front door and they left, locking it behind them.

"I want to thank you for today," she told him as they walked. "I don't think I've had a more relaxing day of shopping ever."

"I liked it, too," he said as he moved his right hand over her left hand. His touch felt right; she thought about what he had said of the hand being the most sensual part of the human body.

"Are you ready for food?" she asked. "We could go eat before we scoot around town."

"I'm ready for food," he said. "How about you?"

"I'm dying for a bowl of clam chowder. The Shell

has an excellent recipe."

They sat at a corner table where everyone there was clearly visible. Their light faire was delivered, along with tall glasses of a local beer. They talked, they watched, and they ate their food with enthusiasm. When they had consumed all they could, they sat back and laughed at one another.

"Those steamers were the best," Luke said. "Are we ready to walk this off?"

Catherine finished her last sip of beer and stood. "Ready."

They left the café on the edge of town and walked throughout the beach strip, the area well lit from neon signs and rows of white strung lights and colorful Japanese lanterns. Had it not been such a strenuous task looking for Trini, this place could easily be construed as occasional fun.

Luke walked with his hands tucked into his trouser pockets. Catherine moved by his side, her hands grasping the wide strap of her shoulder purse as she glanced at each oncoming face and into each shop. She knew the area well, that the scuba gear store was next to the funky jewelry and joke shop. She knew that the dress shop where she'd purchased the black dress Luke favored was next in line to the hat and sunglass shop. She wondered how many of these places had been visited by her sister. She could imagine the attractive young girl wearing a colorful bikini, or bright sunglasses too large for her young face. It kept her heart pounding, always vigilant, searching for the ghost of her family.

As they neared Catherine's cottage, Luke reached

for her key.

"I'll be okay," she said.

"I'd like to see you inside," he insisted.

Catherine gave him the key and he unlocked the door, holding it open for her to enter first. He stepped in right behind her as she flipped a switch adding dim light to the tasteless room. Luke walked to the kitchen, to the bathroom and bedroom then returned.

"Everything seems okay," he said.

Catherine nodded.

Luke moved closer to her and placed his hands at her shoulders, his face close to hers. Catherine moved backward a step and Luke dropped his hands to his pockets. He looked down at her with a pensive smile.

"Does my former vocation make you second-think knowing someone like me?"

Catherine was stunned with the question. "No, not really," she said.

Luke raised his eyebrows and smiled. "And what does 'not really' really mean?"

Catherine moved away from him, leaving her purse to hang on a doorknob. "Want some tea?" she asked.

"No, thank you."

She turned and faced him. "I don't think of you as a former priest, Luke. If I'd known you back then, maybe I would. But meeting you as I have, no, I'm not affected."

Luke nodded. "Okay, then what's going on with us? Something isn't quite right, is it?"

She took a deep and noticeable breath. "It's just going to be difficult once you're gone."

At that point, Luke walked toward her and took her

hand. He led her to the sofa where they sat down - both of them staring at the dingy carpet.

"You know I wouldn't leave if I didn't have to," he said. "And I'd drag you right along with me if you weren't on a mission here. The last thing I want is to leave you here in this tiny cottage where you've already experienced an invasion. I don't think I can properly explain how much I hate this, Catherine."

Catherine leaned back against the sofa, her eyes to the ceiling.

Luke looked at her and then leaned back, his right arm touching her left arm and shoulder. "I wish I had a magic wand to make Trini appear and your worries go away."

Catherine looked at him. "I know."

"Do you also know how important you are to me? I'm not kidding, Catherine. If you weren't immersed in this investigation, I'd literally become a caveman and drag you off. There isn't going to be a single day when I don't talk to you at least once. I'm not leaving you. I'm going to work. My going will not be the end. It will not."

Catherine felt the warm tears fill her eyes. "Okay," she said, and then he wrapped his arms around her in a long and firm embrace.

Before Luke left her that night, he seemed determined not to rush the romantics but to enforce the image of support. "I want every day we have left to be special," he told her. "We'll continue to feed our gulls, search for Trini, and have some fun. Every day, Catherine, I want that for each of us. Does that sound okay to you?"

141

"Yes," she said, "it does. And as soon as you go back, you'll talk to your friend about Trini, right? I'm anxious to know what else he's learned."

"The moment I learn anything, I'll call you. It might not be anything significant, but I promise, I'll call you immediately."

Catherine felt unnerved by what else there might be but, as Luke said, it might be nothing that would add to the search. She tried to relax; she felt stress in every muscle and bone. Trini was nearby, but where? Living in this cottage, devoid of comfort, and then physically tiring herself with the ceaseless search, Catherine cautioned herself about becoming undone. Luke's departure would add to her stress. He was, from the moment she first saw him, magically magnetic. There was no explanation. Without him, she felt certain that she could collapse – that air might leave her lungs.

"I'm going," he said as he stood. "You need some rest, but tomorrow I'll pick up the coffee and something for us and the gulls."

Catherine stood and Luke gently pulled her to him. Giving her hair a tug, he kissed her firmly then left.

Catherine locked the door then leaned against it. It was going to be unbearable without him.

Chapter Ten

With morning light flowing freely into her room, Catherine squinted and wondered what she was hearing. She tossed the coverlet and sheet aside and sat up on the edge of her bed. She stood and walked to the window where she could see a man working at a pipe coming from the green cottage.

After pulling on a pair of jeans and a dark shirt, Catherine slid her feet into sandals and walked outside.

"Excuse me," she said to the man, "is everything all right over here?"

The sixty-something man turned around and eyed Catherine from head to toe. "Yup," he said, "just disconnecting the water. The owner won't rent this place any more this season. Can't have the winter freeze the pipes, you know. That gets expensive if they burst."

Catherine pushed her unruly hair back from her face and wished she had Luke's ability to braid.

"No one else will be living there?" she asked.

"Not this year," he said.

The man returned to his work and Catherine backed away, then she walked into her cottage. So they were gone for good. She couldn't help but think of the dark-haired girl – what had become of her? For whatever reason, she hadn't liked the look of the fair-haired young man she'd watched coming and going. His facial expression seemed harsh, as if he had no feelings for the girl he roughly handled. Catherine worried that Trini could fall victim to a man like that, and she wondered, why did young women all over the world allow this type of intervention? Why did so many men think it was okay to mistreat the very people they yearned for? That, Catherine reasoned, was why she had never told anyone, no one, except her pets and her father when he was dying, that she loved them. Love was dangerous, it made you vulnerable. Then what was this she felt for Luke? She knew, but she refused to speak the words.

Catherine put water on for tea then walked back into her bedroom. She brushed her hair and looked at the small alarm clock on her nightstand. It was not quite eight. She had three full hours before meeting Luke. *Why wait?* She made a cup of tea and left it to steep, then walked across the street. She was about to knock on his door when she could hear a voice from inside.

"I can't do that to her," she heard Luke speak in a muted voice. "No," he continued, "I can't. She's unsuspecting. She would have no reason to think of me in any other way. I can't do it."

Catherine heard the receiver go back into place and held her breath. What was Luke talking about? What was he capable of keeping from her and who was 'her'? Catherine backed away from the door, covered her mouth then ran back to her cottage. Inside she grabbed her purse and keys, locked the door and bolted to the car. She started the engine, backed the car into the street, and as fast as she could, drove away.

In minutes she was passing the rocky coast and the waiting gulls. She cried and kept going. More than an hour later, she stopped for gas then drove on until she found herself in Connecticut. Exhausted and disappointed in her poor judgment, she pulled into a drive-thru and bought herself a cup of coffee. She sat in the parking lot drinking it until after eleven. She felt immobilized. What had Luke done to her? What part was he playing in this miserable search? Catherine had never felt so alone. How could she be so wrong about her feelings for Luke? She thought about his declaration of being a fraud.

She drove further and, after several hours, reversed her direction. She made two more stops just to use up time. After a third stop, she bought more coffee and headed back toward the beach. It was getting dark – she needed to walk that strip and look for Trini; that had not changed.

Catherine did not return her car to the cottage. She didn't want to go anywhere near where Luke would see her. She parked in the police station parking lot and walked a distance to reach the familiar beach street where she was hopeful she'd see Trini appear.

Fatigued and frightened, heartbroken over Luke's betrayal, Catherine walked the streets and wanted to sink to the curb. She wondered if anything in her entire life had ever felt this bad. Riley's cancer, her father's death and disclosure of having a child, nothing had felt this grave.

Catherine stopped walking for a moment and leaned against a doorway. She closed her eyes and wished she could so easily shut out her emotions.

145

"Catherine, for God's sake, where have you been?" Luke scolded with a face showing stress.

Catherine opened her eyes and stared at him. She said nothing and he reached for her hand.

"Don't," she said as she started to walk toward the cottage and then stopped as she remembered her car wasn't there.

"Catherine. What in hell is going on? I've been worried sick. You need to give me your cell number, and I'll give you mine. This is ridiculous. I was going crazy all day. Where have you been?"

She pulled away from him and started to walk toward the police station.

Luke followed, keeping up with her fast pace. "Stop," he said as he placed a large hand over her arm. "What's going on, Catherine?"

She turned to him, tears streaming over her face. "Why, Luke? Why have you been deceiving me?"

"What? Catherine, I've never deceived you, I never would. What are you saying?"

She turned and continued to walk.

"Would you mind telling me where in hell we're going?"

"To the police station," she said.

"Why? What's happened?"

"I left my car there to avoid seeing you," she said.

"Great. Thanks. What did I do to deserve this wrath? Come on, Catherine. You owe me an explanation."

When they reached Catherine's car she unlocked it. Luke placed his hand over hers.

"Let go of me," she said, "or I'll scream and bring

146

the whole damn department out here."

Luke tightened his grasp. "Go ahead. Bring on the U.S. Army! I'm not budging until you tell me what's going on."

Catherine shook her hand from his and glared at him. "I heard you this morning. You were apparently on the phone. I went over to see if you wanted to go earlier for breakfast. I heard you, Luke. I heard you telling someone about keeping things from me."

Luke put his hands over his eyes. "Oh, my God, Catherine," he said as he dropped his hands to his sides. "I was talking to my father in Florida. He wants me to level with my aunt. He thinks I'm doing her an injustice. I wasn't talking about you, Catherine, not until I told him I was completely saturated in love."

Catherine gasped and ran her hand over her tear-stained face. She looked at him and then felt the salty, warm tears flow again. She closed her eyes and felt herself being pulled into his arms.

With her eyes closed and her face against his shoulder, Catherine could hear his strong, rapid heartbeat.

"Have we come so far, Catherine, and yet not found trust? I can't believe what's happened today. The only thing good that came of this is that I now understand your intense need to search for your sister. I thought I was going to lose my mind when you didn't show up at the rocks. I saw that your car was gone, but figured you'd had an errand to run early. When it got to be noon, I knew something was wrong; you're never late."

Catherine pushed gently away from him and

momentarily closed her eyes. "I'm sorry," she said softly.

Luke stuffed his hands in his pockets as she slipped into her car. She started the engine, put the car in reverse then looked up at Luke. "Do you want a ride back?"

He looked at her with pain etched on his handsome face. "No," he said, then he turned and began to walk.

Catherine watched him walk away, his lean back to her as she kept her foot on the brake. She put the car in park and sat there, then she looked at the brightened windows of the police station. She dried her eyes and turned off the engine. With her keys and purse in her hand, she got out of the car and walked inside. A different clerk was working at the desk and looked up as Catherine entered.

"Can I help you, ma'am?" he asked.

"I was curious about something I left here a while ago. It was a necklace. I just wondered if anyone had claimed it."

The clerk took her name and checked his computer screen.

"A sapphire and diamond necklace?" he asked.

"Yes," she said of the blue and clear stones.

"It's still here, ma'am. But we did send the information and a picture of it out through the system; nothing yet."

"Okay, thank you," she said as she turned to the door. In her car, she looked around for any sign of Luke. He was nowhere in sight. She started her engine and drove back to the cottage.

Inside, feeling wilted from the agonizing day,

Catherine locked the door and with her purse still on her shoulder, she sank into the faded sofa and sobbed. What had she done to Luke? She wished she could go to sleep. She wanted to forget what she'd heard that morning and the senseless journey she'd gone on to avoid what was the best thing in her life. Now she'd injured him - the last thing in the world she would ever want to do.

Unable to rest, Catherine left her purse on the sofa and walked to the kitchen. The cup of cold tea sat there from the morning. She stared at it thinking that she might heat it up and drink it then she poured it down the drain and took a warm shower. She changed into a knee-length nightdress and climbed beneath the sheet and coverlet, pulling them up to her chin. She reached over to the lamp next to her bed, switched it off and closed her eyes - numb for what she had relinquished – Luke.

When morning came, it was with the understanding that now everything was different. No more breakfasts on the rocks. No more walking the beach strip with someone at her side. No energy for anything other than breathing.

Catherine walked in bare feet to the front window and looked across to Luke's cottage. His car was there. When she looked again an hour later, it was gone. Had he left for the rocks? She couldn't face him. Instead, she dressed and then drove out of town to a coffee shop where she bought tea and an English muffin. She drank the tea and ate half of the muffin in her car, wondering how to spend the remainder of the day. She wanted it all to disappear, to just fade into night so that she could

149

do the only thing she knew how to do, walk and search.

By four in the afternoon, Catherine had been sitting listlessly for hours in her car. She drove back to the cottage and noted that Luke's car was not in front of his place. She wondered where he was. Had she driven him off to Vermont prematurely? With his aunt gone, he had no reason to stay, except for, as he'd insinuated, Catherine. She wanted to cry until there wasn't a drop of fluid left in her body. No one had ever made her feel this way before. She went into her cottage, walked around the small space, then sat in her rocking chair. She would wait until dusk and then she would walk. She had no choice; she couldn't give up on Trini.

Two more days passed in exactly the same way. Catherine checked from her window to see if Luke's car was there. Early in the day, yes – later in the morning, no. At eleven, she drove past the area where they were accustomed to parking. His car was there – she kept going.

On the day that he had intended to leave, Catherine drove to the rocks and parked her car next to Luke's. She took a deep breath and buttoned her light jacket, then she walked across the street to the stairway down to where he sat, facing the sea, tossing bread to the gulls. She resisted crying. She had no idea what she was going to say to him, but she walked toward him and then sat down next to his cup of coffee.

Luke didn't look at her. She looked at his handsome profile and could see the sadness there. She'd done this to him, to this sweet, wonderful, completely remarkable man.

"Are you leaving today?" she asked in a half

whisper.

"Yes," he said without looking at her.

Catherine swallowed hard and looked to the sea, following his eyes and the swooping gulls.

"I didn't mean to mistrust you, Luke. It was so stupid of me to assume that you were talking about me. I'm so messed up with this business of being on edge all the time. I'm sorry. Please forgive me," she cried.

"Why?" he asked, and then he looked into her blue eyes, moist and red with tears. "Does this relationship really matter to you, Catherine? Have I been totally blind and dumb about this whole thing? I convinced myself that we were together."

Catherine drew her knees up to her chin, covered her eyes and cried.

Luke stood and started to move away.

Catherine scrambled to her feet and ran to catch up to him with his long strides. "Luke," she said in a voice barely audible, "Luke, don't leave me."

He stopped walking, turned around to face her then reached for her, holding her breathlessly tight. After several silent moments, except for the roar of the ocean and the cry of the gulls, Luke looked at her beautiful face.

"I'm not leaving you, Catherine."

"But your work," she said in a strangled voice.

He kissed her lightly then said, "I do need to go to work, but I'm not leaving you. You and I are not leaving one another, not now, not ever. I'm going to talk to you every day, probably way too many times every day. And when this is through, and I hope that's soon, I want you to get in your car and drive to

151

Vermont. Whether I stay there long-term or I end up back here, I want you with me. Are you listening to me, Catherine?"

"We're not leaving one another," she said.

"That's right," he whispered and then he kissed her long and hard.

When he loosened his grip enough that she could look into his dark eyes she said, "I want something."

"Oh, really? And what is that?"

"I want," she said, "you."

Luke looked at her and smiled. "Was that a proposition I just heard?"

"Yes."

Without so much as a blink of his eyes, Luke asked, "Where?"

They checked into a small, pretty little coastal hotel and didn't mind that the clerk at the desk had a smile on his face as he passed them a key for room seventeen.

From the window in their cozy room, they faced the ocean and a stretch of sand dotted with tufts of pale grass; it was Catherine who made the first move. With her purse slung onto a chair, she unbuttoned her jacket and tossed it on top of the purse. She slipped the sandals off her otherwise bare feet and then unsnapped and unzipped her jeans. Luke watched. She walked over to him and put her hands at his waist. She unbuttoned his black shirt, pulling it from where the trousers wrestled with her fingers. She unbuckled his belt then reached up with her hands to his face.

Stretched over and around one another in an ample bed, Catherine felt relaxed and content in his arms, her head against his heart. Luke kept his right arm under and around her, his left hand draped over her left hip. He held her to him as they enjoyed the silky sheets and the late afternoon light filtering through the room. Catherine's eyes traveled the peach colored draperies at the window then moved to the peach and green shades in the intricate pattern of the rug.

"Is your synesthesia kicking in?" Luke asked with a smile. "I can see you're enjoying the details of this place."

"My synesthesia," she said squeezing him lightly, "doesn't need to 'kick in' – it's always on duty. Sometimes I feel almost ashamed of what I take in on a daily basis. I love what I notice; it's a shame that everyone doesn't experience what I do."

"You should be a poet," he said. "You could write some great little sonnets about what you see."

Catherine smiled. "I've done that. As a teenager, I didn't know what to do with my conglomeration of thoughts. I wrote, I sketched, I made bouquets out of weird little combinations of grasses and found them beautiful – I did it all. With synesthesia, it's about more than the visuals though. It's how you perceive sounds, good music becomes wonderful music. Loud sounds become obnoxious. Soft fabrics feel necessary; scratchy fabrics are a toss-away. Everything is enhanced."

Luke gave her a playful squeeze. "How about *us*?"

Catherine smiled and moved to position herself so that her lips were less than an inch from his. "Let me see if I can better explain myself *this* way."

When they had showered and dressed, it was decided they should have something to eat and then head out for their nightly walk into town. The air was heavy with a predicted rainstorm and, although there were people wandering the streets, there were not nearly as many as usual. It gave Catherine the opportunity to more closely scrutinize faces and shops, bars and cafés. Still, there was nothing to indicate Trini's presence.

Back at Catherine's cottage near midnight, Luke held her close and she invited him in.

"I'd like nothing better," he said, "but I need to hit the road."

"Tonight?" she asked as she looked up into his handsome face.

"I need to be there for a meeting at ten in the morning. I have to go."

Catherine felt weak from the thought of his leaving, but she had known from the beginning that he couldn't stay. She leaned her forehead into his chest and then looked at him and smiled. "I'm glad we had today," she said, "and all our days. The day at the mall was wonderful. You've been a Godsend to me."

Luke hugged her close. "Maybe that's what people mean when they talk about God's divine intervention. Maybe this is what my true calling was about - finding you, you finding me."

Catherine wanted to cry, but she didn't. They exchanged cell phone numbers. She used every ounce of strength to smile, hug him back, and tell him to drive carefully. Standing in her doorway, she watched him walk across the street to his car, which was already packed and ready to go; she felt that the earth had dropped away from her feet. The red taillights glimmered in the dark, starless night. Catherine walked into her cottage, flipping a switch to illuminate the room just enough to maneuver about. She sat down on the sofa, her jacket still on, her purse in her lap. She closed her eyes and emotionally rode with Luke on his four-hour journey to Vermont.

An hour later, her phone rang.

"Hello," she said, expecting to hear her mother's voice from Arizona where it was no later than nine o'clock.

"I miss you already," he said.

Catherine sat up straight on the sofa then smiled. "Where are you?"

"In Massachusetts, about to pick up Route 93 toward New Hampshire. I'll be an hour and a half on 93, then I'll cut over onto 89 and head to Vermont."

"I wish I was with you," she said. "You know I would be."

"I know," he said. "But Catherine, please be careful. People are going to see you wandering around on your own, and you don't know who is watching who. Please, if you even slightly suspect anyone has entered your place, don't go in. Promise me."

"I promise you," she said with a smile. "Don't forget that I was a police officer and I do have a black belt."

"All it takes is one bullet, Catherine. Please, stay in your police officer mentality. Don't forget how dangerous some people can be."

They talked for several minutes about what Luke had in store for the next day. He had planned meetings, settling back into his home on campus, and dinner with

Charlie, who had more information regarding Trini and her mother.

"I'll call you tonight, my love," Luke ended his call.

Catherine held the now silent phone in her hands and looked at the clock. It was after two in the morning – it would be at least eighteen long hours before she could expect to hear from Luke again.

She thought about staying on the sofa then decided to go to her bed. She looked at the darkened cottage next door, unable to shake the concern she felt for the young woman who had spent her summer there. How was she? *Where* was she?

Catherine pulled the shade down and changed into a pair of jersey slacks and a t-shirt to sleep. She lay back and embraced her pillow as if leaning against Luke, and then she slept.

When she woke in the morning, the day was gray and there were rivulets of rain against the windowpane. Catherine slipped out of bed, pulled the covers up in order, then walked to the kitchen to make tea. She returned to her room and dressed, then she sat down on her bed and thought how this was a lonely time without the prospect of seeing Luke. She went to the bakery in town where she bought two loaves of day-old bread for the gulls and a coffee for herself. She was on the rocks in a gentle mist by ten o'clock and she remained there until noon. The gulls were grateful for their extra helping of bread and Catherine was thankful for their companionship.

She thought about Luke's question, where did these adept flyers sleep at night? They were the consummate survivors, able to navigate land and sea, a constant endeavor to sustain. People, she thought, could take a lesson from their resilience.

Catherine pulled her knees up to her chin as she sat on the rocks. As wonderful as this place was, with its endless surf and crashing waves, without Luke, it was just the sea. In the most unlikely of circumstances and locations, she had found the love of her life. She ached for the moment when she could hold him in her arms again. With no prospect for that immersing sensation in the near future, Catherine swallowed a sip of coffee and decided to go back to town. She spoke aloud to the gulls, telling them to stay safe, and then she walked to her car.

Back at the cottage, she changed her shirt, damp with the light rain, and slipped on a light jacket over a red t-shirt. She walked into town, bought a large pretzel from a vendor, then strolled slowly in and out of shops, showing Trini's picture when it seemed like the right person and timing. Out of more than nine shop owners, only one indicated that he had seen Trini. This summer, Catherine asked? Yes, this summer, earlier in the season. Nice girl, polite, not rowdy like some.

Instinctively, Catherine knew this about her sister. Trini would not be the usual little summer butterfly. She had been known as a hard worker, reliable with children. She had been spoken of as being sweet and gentle, smart and soft-spoken, and perhaps easily led. Catherine sighed with a yearning to find her. There was so much she could tell her about their father. Yes, he'd made his mistakes, but there was more to him than a brief affair. He'd been the one who taught Catherine to

157

read at the age of four. He was tireless in his effort to teach her right from wrong. He was the quintessential police officer, taking his work to heart. Catherine wanted Trini to know this. She wanted Trini to know that she had a sister who cared.

By three in the afternoon, Catherine had walked the town at least four times. Weaving her way through handholding couples, their arms touching; she could remember that burning, stirring sensation of being next to Luke. Since that first day seeing him in black, then noticing the white patch at his throat, she had inexplicably been intrigued by him.

Rather than return to her cottage before nightfall, Catherine walked into a small café and ordered a meal. As she sat poking at a salad and a small bowl of pasta, she was approached three times by attractive men of varying ages. She told each one of them that she was passing time waiting for her husband.

With moistened, darkened streets glimmering in neon colors and pale street lights, Catherine walked. She'd been accustomed to this steady aloneness before Luke began to join her in the search, but now he was gone and the sifting through of faces, shops, and bars had become more than a chore. It was a solitary struggle with only hope as her guide.

She consulted her watch at eleven and wondered when she would hear from Luke. She started to walk toward the cottage when the phone rang. She stopped, said hello, then heard his voice and felt both soothed and anxious.

"Anything on Trini?" she asked.

"A bit. Where are you?"

"Walking back to the cottage. I've been in town all day – nothing."

"Call me when you get in and we'll talk."

"Luke, what does that mean? Is there something significant?"

"It's not huge, Catherine, but I'd like you to get in and check the place out. Please call me as you're putting the key in the lock. It's driving me to distraction having you there on your own."

Catherine smiled. "I was here on my own for weeks before you came on the scene," she said softly but sternly.

"I know, I know," he said. "Please, indulge me."

"Okay. I'll call you in about ten minutes. I miss you."

"I don't even know how to explain how I feel," he said. "But to put it mildly, I miss you, too - tremendously."

They disconnected and Catherine picked up her pace. It was cold and raw with a gusting wind. Although the rain had stopped, it left everything feeling heavy with moisture, including Catherine's long hair. It brought to mind even more that autumn was near. She would be forced to move and, if she didn't find Trini soon, be left with no information on her sister; the thought of that made Catherine shiver. How could she learn she had a sibling and have no opportunity to at least meet her, talk with her?

Inside the cottage, Catherine left her jacket and purse on the sofa and sat down in her rocking chair. She dialed Luke's number and he picked up immediately.

"Everything okay there?" he asked.

"Yes, everything's okay. Is there news about Trini?"

"Well," Luke said, "it's not anything that will aid in your search, but it's interesting. Did you know that your sister's name is Trinity, not just Trini?"

Catherine frowned. "No, I only heard her name as Trini."

"Her birth certificate lists her as Trinity Maria Bauer. And, of course, her mother was Helga Bauer. The interesting part is that your sister had two brothers born to Helga when she was eighteen. Trini was born to Helga at the age of twenty-two. Apparently the boys were raised by a grandmother, Helga's adoptive mother, and that's when Helga came to the states as a nanny."

"Trini has two brothers," Catherine said in a low, trance-like voice.

"She did. They were four years older than Trini, Hans and Eric, identical twins."

Catherine's left hand went over her mouth. She was stunned.

"Catherine, are you all right?"

She took her hand away from her mouth and switched the cell phone into that hand. "Yes. I'm just surprised with this information. Where are the twins?"

"I don't know. But that may account for why Helga named her daughter Trinity; she completed the triangle of three with an appropriate name."

Catherine closed her eyes for a moment and sighed. "I never considered that there were other siblings for Trini. This is mindboggling."

"There's one more thing. It seems the boys

resented their sister because she was half-American."

"They don't sound particularly nice," Catherine said.

Luke sighed. "I wish I had the ability to be with you through this."

They spoke about their day, Catherine's visit to the gulls and Luke's meetings and preparations for classes. They were two separate entities with one compatible mission, to be together.

Chapter Eleven

Catherine thought about her sister that night until she fell asleep. She woke in the morning thinking about her again. That Trini had twin brothers was news to Catherine. She wondered if her father had known that Helga left Germany and her sons behind in her quest to be a nanny in the United States. If he'd been aware, he had not revealed that information to Catherine's mother whose personality was such that she would not have left that leaf unturned. She would have questioned, what mother leaves her children and goes to a foreign country?

Before eleven, Catherine bought coffee and bread. She sat on the rocks and felt incredibly lonely, for Luke and for all of her life, which seemed to have tolerated but not tended to her. Perhaps now she had a chance. Between the hope of finding Trini and the fierce longing for Luke, Catherine had a purpose.

Watching the gulls, she smiled. How polite they were, half dancing on the rocks, their feet soaked in the salty sea. They seemed to be ever so cautious about not infringing on one another's space. Some were aggressive while others were timid – just like people. Luke, she decided, must miss them. He was a thoughtful man, one who cared about others even if they were feathered and slightly screechy. She had no doubts that he'd been an exemplary priest and that his decision to leave had not come easy. He was a complete package with great looks, logic and sweet thoughts. She smiled thinking about being with him – it had been natural, as if they'd been waiting all their lives for one another, that they had never been anything except together.

Leaving the rocks before two, Catherine drove to her cottage and then walked into town. She'd skipped breakfast and was ready for food.

She walked toward The Shell, then reconsidered because the restaurant would remind her too much of a memorable evening with Luke; instead she walked to a café in the town's center. She chose her seating so that she could see the room and the doorway, just in case. There was never a time when she ceased to look for Trini. Every blonde, every braid, every young woman was scrutinized carefully.

Catherine ordered iced tea and a tuna salad sandwich on toasted rye. People walked in to pick up orders waiting in brown paper bags and the pungent odor of sautéed onions filled the small room. She ate slowly as the place wasn't busy; she didn't mind lingering over lunch as she scanned the doorway for a sign of her sister. It was so much nicer when Luke was at her side. He'd managed to soften the search, to distract her enough so that she wasn't saturated with stress. She missed him terribly.

Standing and starting to leave, her cell phone rang. She thought it might be her mother, but it was Luke. She sat down again.

"Hi," she said. "The seagulls miss you. I think you

should come back to see them."

Luke laughed. "I intend to as soon as I can. How are you?"

"I'm okay, how about you?"

"I'm lonely. Other than that, okay. I had a decent day – met some of the students, classes officially begin tomorrow."

They were quiet, neither of them finding it necessary to speak, just as when they were at the sea on their rocks.

"Are you really all right?" he asked after a few moments.

Catherine rubbed her forehead with her fingers then sat back in her chair. "I'm a little worn down, but I can't stop."

"I know you can't," he said. "It's perplexing not to have caught even a glimpse of Trini."

"Trinity," Catherine said. "That name makes her sound so serious, maybe even religious."

"We don't know yet what she's like, but since she goes by Trini, it sounds like she's rearranged her name to be comfortable with it. I keep thinking I'd like her."

Catherine smiled. "Yeah, me too."

Again, they were silent. Being connected by phone was enough for the moment. It had to be.

"Where are you?" he asked. "I hear dishes clanking around."

"I'm in a little hole in the wall. I had coffee on the rocks with our gulls, but I skipped food. I stopped in this little place for a sandwich. I was just about to leave when you called."

"I suppose you're going out to wander the streets

again tonight."

Catherine nodded then said, "Yes."

"You'll be careful."

She smiled. "I will."

"Could you give me a call when you get in later?"

"Of course," she said. "I will if you want me to. I don't want to wake you though; you know I stay out pretty late."

"I know. That's okay."

As she walked the streets later, she heard a distant church bell chime twelve times. The crowd had thinned over the past two weeks. Catherine looked around and found herself to be one of not more than a dozen people still in the street.

As she passed a closed shop, she noticed a young, desperately thin girl crouched in the doorway ravenously eating a slice of pizza, as if she hadn't eaten in days. Catherine guessed the girl to be in her teens, maybe seventeen or younger. It made Catherine want to cry, thinking that Trini could be existing this way. If only she could make contact to at least give her some cash. Catherine wasn't well off, but she'd lived simply and saved for the ultimate rainy days. She could afford to share with her sister.

Catherine walked by the girl then hesitated. She turned around and walked back to her.

"Are you all right?" she asked.

The girl, her eyes seeming huge in her thin face, looked up at Catherine and said nothing. Catherine reached into her purse for a twenty-dollar bill, which she placed in the girl's lap. There was no thank you, no response at all, but Catherine hoped it would be cash for a meal rather than another round of drugs.

A few doors from where the girl perched, perhaps for the night, Catherine saw two men arguing in the middle of the street. Their voices weren't raised, but it was obvious to anyone that they were in disagreement by their rough talk and gestures. Catherine slowed her pace to observe, her police experience kicking in. She was shocked when the man with his back to her moved enough that she could see he was the light-haired neighbor from the cottage next door. She wondered where he was living now that he'd relinquished the cottage. And she again thought of the girl who had been living there with him – was she even still alive?

Resolved to end her search for that day, Catherine walked toward the cottage where she called Luke and spoke to him just long enough to say goodnight.

"I love you," he said.

Catherine closed her eyes for a moment. "I miss you," she replied.

For an hour after speaking with Luke, Catherine sat on the sofa, her mind spinning with all she had seen and what she was thinking. Not having Luke to walk and talk with was a hardship. Seeing the young girl in the doorway was heartbreaking – someone must wonder where she is, Catherine thought – maybe parents, maybe a sister. She had a rescue attitude, as if she wanted to go out and drag these young kids in to a safe place, physically and emotionally. As a police officer, she understood that much of what she saw was not preventable or correctable by her; it was a matter of timing and choice for these kids to pick themselves up and move on.

Catherine took a shower and went to bed. She fell asleep and was surprised in the morning that with all she had on her mind, rest had found her and she was feeling refreshed. She made the usual trip to town for bread, coffee and a scone.

Later, Catherine decided to take a break and drove onto the highway toward the city mall thirty miles away. Nearing the exit where she and Luke traveled, it almost made her ill to think of being there without him. She passed the exit and, when it was convenient, she turned the car onto a ramp heading back toward the beach. At the sharp curve entering the highway, Catherine took note of a grassy patch of land and a flock of Canada Geese grazing near the busy road. She hoped for their safety, but she also observed the triangular shaped terrain – she understood that it was her synesthesia, but she found that space, as did the geese, alluring. She thanked whoever created that miniscule slice of green and gold earth; it was beautiful in the afternoon sun.

Arriving back at the beach strip by four in the afternoon, Catherine was vigilant about keeping her eyes on the young women roaming about, but she was also feeling despondent. The search for Trini was routine – nothing of significance had become apparent. Those who seemed to recognize the young blonde were reluctant or unable to supply any useful information. That they had seen her was not helpful. When they were turning away from Catherine's questions, it presented another issue. Catherine could not seem to be the police, and she could not seem to be someone who would intentionally harm Trini. Her friends and

167

acquaintances would protect her. Unless Catherine was fortunate enough to catch a glimpse of her sister, the odds were not favorable toward a positive outcome. She had not expected it to be this hard.

Carefully, slowly, she drove down the main strip, stopping and starting to avoid pedestrians. Back at the cottage she sighed and looked in the rear-view mirror to tidy her hair. She sat there for a few moments, her eyes drawn to Luke's empty cottage diagonally across the street. This place had not seemed particularly friendly to her before she met Luke and, since his departure, it was incredibly lonely. Catherine reasoned that meeting him, knowing him, had saved her sanity. A summer saturated in only the hunt for her sister would have been unbearable. Luke had turned a part of each day into companionship and pure wonder.

She turned off the engine and opened her car door, sliding out into the sunshine. Reluctantly, she walked to the door, unlocked it, then went inside and looked around. Everything was in order. Catherine left her purse on the sofa then walked into the kitchen. She drew a glass of water from the faucet and returned to the rocking chair in the front room to sit and think. Where could she go that would be different? Walking the street, in and out of shops and cafés had proved nothing. Where would someone twenty-two like to go? And if they didn't dare to go at all, where would they stay and with whom?

As she sat, her eyes closed, one knee drawn up to her chest, the phone rang. Catherine moved toward her purse and phone and smiled as she saw that it was Luke.

"Hi," she said with obvious joy in her voice.

"Hi," he said. "Have I told you I hate the distance between us?"

Catherine laughed. "I think so and, in case you wonder, I hate it, too."

"What did you do today?"

"I had brunch with the gulls and then I drove, out of pure madness, toward the city mall. I don't know what I thought I was escaping – thoughts and memories follow us around. I was nearly there when I turned the car around and came back to the cottage."

"No shopping trips today?"

"Not without you."

"That's hopeful," he said, "I think I like that."

"How's school? Should I be worried about the attractive young women in your classes?"

"I think most of them are in good health," he said. "They sure look healthy."

Catherine smiled. "If you were here, I'd give you a punch."

"I don't think you have to worry about my students," he said, "or anyone else."

Catherine moved back to her rocking chair and sat down. She shifted in her seat and sighed.

"I heard that," he said. "Are you tired?"

"I'm a little weary I guess. I'm not as optimistic about finding Trini as when I first arrived here. It's so hard, Luke. I keep wondering where she could be. Unless someone is shielding her, she needs to come out of hiding to eat. My hope is to catch that one time, but what if she doesn't need to reveal herself? It's very possible that a friend is delivering food to her. It's horrible; I think of all the possibilities and it's driving me to distraction."

"It's unlikely that she'd be staying in a public place, so you're right, she could be staying where no one would see her. Having two men looking for her, she could be afraid for her safety. However, have you actually gone to the police? You could level with them about being her sister. You never know; they could have some information on her."

Catherine frowned. "I haven't gone to them except to leave the necklace, but you're right, it wouldn't be harmful to talk to them. I could even show them her photo. I'll walk the strip tonight and if I see nothing of her again, tomorrow I'll go to the police. That's really a good idea, Luke. I've been trying so hard to avoid *being* the police, but I could try to enlist their help. They might not divulge anything for reasons of protocol, but then again they might cooperate knowing my background and that I am Trini's sister."

"I wish I was with you," he said. "I have a stack of lessons to get through tonight, I'll be up all hours. Please call me when you get in from the strip. It drives me nuts having you out walking around alone in that atmosphere."

"I'll be fine," she said.

"I suppose you will," he said, "but it doesn't stop me from worrying. People will take advantage of you, Catherine; you're too attractive."

"Really?" she teased. "I didn't know that clergymen, or *former* clergymen, had such observations."

"I'm spanking you when I get hold of you," he

170

said.

"Ooh," Catherine teased. "I had no idea you could be so innovative."

"You," he said, "are in trouble when I see you."

Catherine laughed. "Which is when?"

"I have meetings and a seminar this weekend, but if you're still there in a week and a half, I might try for an overnight. The only problem is I no longer have a cottage to stay in."

Catherine bit her lower lip. "Hmm," she began, "that's a problem all right."

"I think we'll work something out," he said. "But in the meanwhile, please, Catherine, don't take any risks. It's not going to do Trini any good if something happens to you. Promise me, no taking chances."

"I promise."

When their call ended, Catherine sat with the phone in her hands. She had been reluctant to know him for fear of a heart-wrenching summer love. She and Luke seemed to have found one another at a time when they each had needs. She wanted more than anything to tell him that from the first moment she saw him, even before he turned and she saw his handsome face, she was captivated. What was that about? How could you see someone, know nothing about them, and not care who they were except for being a mysterious part of your heart? She was concerned that her good common sense had deserted her.

Catherine entertained thoughts of not going into town this one time. She was tired and discouraged. She looked at her clothes, changed into something more in line with beach strip fashions, then locked the door and left. She decided to have a sandwich at a little café she had frequented before she met Luke. With a coffee to go she could walk around town pretending to browse in shops where little or nothing held much appeal. Catherine stopped at a boutique that was closed to look in the window. There was something about the place that made her think that Trini would be drawn to these funky, yet classy styles. One pale pink scarf was intriguing, looking like cotton candy with a fringe. She saw a silver shell dangling from a twisted silver chain. These were items Catherine could envision on her sister. Was she imagining Trini's taste, or was it simply the hope of a sibling in search?

Catherine walked on, but she decided that tomorrow she would go to that boutique when it was open. She would show the owner or clerk Trini's picture.

At a shop a few doors down, Catherine stopped to look at jewelry made from tiny shells. It wasn't her taste, but she admired the artistic way in which the items were assembled to create earrings and bracelets. As she started to move away, she noticed the reflection of a man near to her and she turned around.

"Window shopping?" he asked with a broad smile.

Catherine looked at him. He was a good looking forty-something but absolutely not her type. His breath reeked of beer and cheap wine, and his clothing indicated that he was probably driving a motorcycle. A black leather vest served as a shirt and jeans with boots completed his attire.

"I suppose I am," she said.

"I'd be happy to buy you something in there," he

said. "Pretty little lady like you should have pretty things on her body."

Catherine stiffened. "That's very kind of you," she said, "but I buy my own jewelry and, actually, I'm not interested in these except for the effort it took to make them."

He looked at her as if she were speaking a foreign language and his smile faded.

"I guess a lady like you wouldn't want a beer with me, huh?"

"I'm sorry," she lied. "I'm meeting my boyfriend and I'm running late."

Without another word, she walked away. When she was a few doors down from that shop, she turned and saw that he was gone. No doubt he was off looking for another victim.

The creepiness of that man, sneaking up behind her, so willing to buy her a piece of jewelry, gave Catherine a reason to shiver. She crossed the street and stopped at an outdoor bar where she asked to purchase two oranges. From there, she decided she'd had enough and walked back to her cottage.

As usual, she had left the outside light on at her front door. While inserting the key in the lock, she turned and saw that Luke's cottage was dark. No one else had rented it for the remainder of the season. The green cottage next to her had been dark for days. The place was becoming a little spooky. She felt anxious to get inside where she could change into pajamas and call Luke.

Comfortable and sitting on the sofa, she dialed his number. When he said hello, she closed her eyes. She

173

wanted to cry.

"Hi," she said.

"Hi there. Everything okay?"

"I'm fine. I wandered around town for a while. I saw this boutique, and while I don't have a concrete reason, I had this feeling that Trini would like that place. It was kind of weird."

"Don't discount intuition," he said. "It could be you have something. Did you eat?"

"Yes, I had a sandwich and coffee."

"I guess that's better than nothing, or one of your infamous pretzels. I hate having you there alone. I hope this search turns up something soon. I keep thinking that you're going to feel desperate and take risks. I know I harp on this but, Catherine, you're in dangerous territory."

"I'm careful," she said and smiled. "I'm enjoying your nurturing attitude though."

Luke sighed and she heard him.

"Your friend didn't come up with anything else on Helga or Trini, did he?"

"No," Luke replied. "He thought it was a little peculiar, the mother of twins leaving them and going off to be a nanny in another country. She must have felt secure in leaving though. I can't imagine a mother doing that. Why?"

"I've thought that myself. Why would she leave two little boys to take care of other children in a foreign country? And then she gets mixed up with a married man and has his child. There are so many questions reeling around in my mind and I doubt I'll ever have the answers, unless Trini knows."

"That's true," Luke said. "Your sister may be able to fill in the blanks. But I want to talk to you about us. I'm definitely planning to visit you a week from this weekend. We'll feed our gulls and have breakfast at the sea. We'll dine at Ricardo's and we'll have lunch at The Shell. And maybe we'll get to the mall again. I can't wait to see you."

"Wow, are you staying for a week?" she teased.

Luke laughed. "I want us to have a good time."

Catherine smiled and was glad he couldn't see her at that moment, draped in loose-fitting pajamas and bare feet.

"What are you wearing?" he asked.

Catherine sat up straight. "Good Lord," she said, "have I a pervert on the phone?"

"I just want to picture you," he said. "Tell me."

Catherine looked down at her casual attire. "I'm in jersey pajama bottoms and a loose fitting shirt. Satisfied?"

"Sounds pretty nice," he said.

Catherine nearly laughed. "And what do you have on, black something or other?"

"How did you know?"

"Do you really have black on?" she asked.

Luke laughed. "At the moment, I am wearing gray slacks and a blue shirt, school fashion. You know," he said, "you'd like it here. It's beautiful. I have a house on the college grounds as part of the deal. The place is surrounded with maples and oaks, and every morning a warren of wild rabbits hop around the grounds."

"It sounds lovely, but don't you miss the gulls?"

"You know I do. I've decided that this is my work

175

place, but that rocky shore of ours is going to be where I head every chance I get for leisure time."

Catherine sat back and relaxed. "You do know it's nearly one in the morning," she said. "You should probably go to bed."

"And you?"

"I should go to bed also," she said with a smile.

"I'll call you tomorrow. I have a break between classes around one."

"Okay," she said, and then she heard him softly murmur 'I love you' as she closed her eyes and switched off the phone.

Chapter Twelve

When Catherine woke up the next morning, her first thoughts were of Luke. She could envision him as a college professor, the young women swooning over his striking good looks.

She glanced toward the sky from her bed and thought it seemed hazy outside. She would change clothes and go into town for the usual breakfast fare for the gulls and herself; then to the police.

Sitting on the rocks at noon, Catherine found herself hesitant to make the move toward opening her investigation. What if they knew something involving Trini and they began to observe Catherine in her search? She worried that this could occur; she'd seen it happen. Police procedure proclaimed that all was fair in discovery of needed information.

Deciding that she had little choice, Catherine tossed the last of the bread to the gulls and stood, then walked to her car. Once inside, she sat there for a few minutes thinking about how she would explain the situation to the officer or detective on duty. This was not going to be easy.

She started the car and backed out of the space with one last glance toward the sea. She drove past her cottage, slowly through the beach strip of town, looking left to right for a glimpse of her sister. Within minutes, she pulled into the police parking area turning the ignition off. She took a deep breath then stepped out of her car and locked it.

Catherine walked into the small green and white lobby and waited while the clerk explained driving directions to an elderly man. When she stepped up to the window, Catherine asked if there was a detective available. The clerk asked if he was expecting Catherine and she replied that he was not. A call was made and in a few moments, a tall, gray-haired man walked out to the lobby and invited Catherine to step into his office. He offered her coffee, which she declined.

"I'm Detective Jack Stearn, how can I help you?" he asked with a deep voice.

Catherine pulled Trini's picture from her purse. "I'm looking for this girl. I wondered if you were familiar with her and, if so, what you could tell me about her whereabouts."

The detective stared for a long while at the photo then lay it gently down on his desk. "What's your business with this young woman?"

Catherine could tell by his demeanor that he knew of Trini. "I'm looking for her. She's my sister."

The detective raised his ample eyebrows and looked again at Trini's picture.

"When did you last see her?" he asked.

Catherine shifted in her seat. "I haven't seen her," she said.

"In how long?"

"Ever," Catherine admitted.

The detective cocked his head and looked at

Catherine. "This young woman is your sister and you've never seen her?"

"That's right," Catherine said, and then she explained the situation in simple terms.

The detective leaned back in his chair and glanced out at the parking lot through a window to his side. He looked again at Catherine. "I wish I could help you. I know your sister; she's been a regular on the strip for the past two summers. Nice kid, but she hangs out with the wrong crowd. I haven't seen her in weeks."

"But you did see her this summer?" Catherine asked in an anxious tone.

He nodded. "At the beginning of summer, yes. In fact, I warned her to stay away from some of her former cohorts. I doubt she paid much attention, but I tried. I haven't seen her since."

Catherine swallowed back tears. The detective noted Catherine's expression.

"Is she in trouble?" Catherine asked. "I heard people were looking for her."

The detective studied Catherine's beautiful face. "I heard that as well."

"Do you know who's looking for her and why?" Catherine asked.

"I don't know who they are, but I have an idea why. Your sister had an issue with drugs. My guess is she owed money to some unsavory sorts. I can't tell you any more than that. I'm sorry. I can see this is upsetting for you."

Catherine felt the traitorous tears escape from her eyes and she whisked them away as she stood. "Will you let me know if you hear anything at all?" she said

179

as she handed him a card with her name and phone number. "I feel I've exhausted my own ideas for how to locate her. Nothing has worked. And yet I do feel the nearness of her, which probably sounds silly to you."

The detective smiled as he stood and walked Catherine to the door. "Nothing sounds silly to me. We'll keep your name and number on file. If I hear anything at all on Trini Bauer, I'll be in touch."

Catherine thanked the fatherly man and walked out of the station and to her car. She sat inside and rested her forehead against the steering wheel, resolved to continue the search in the only way she could – on foot, through town, hoping for a sighting of Trini. She straightened up and started the car's engine. Driving away from town, she felt the need to escape, to see something different. She drove for about an hour, making a circle in her journey so that she ended up back at the beach by late afternoon. She stopped in town for a sandwich and Coke to go, then drove back to her cottage. Catherine felt weary and insecure about her quest, but she knew that when it was dark, she would walk the strip to observe every detail she might have missed at other times. She wasn't giving up.

When the phone rang, it woke Catherine who had her half-eaten sandwich perched on her lap. It was Luke and she smiled at the prospect of speaking with him.

"Hi," she said sleepily.

"Hi," he said. "You sound a little down, is everything okay? Did you go to the police?"

"I did." She filled him in on the conversation with the detective. "They know her," she concluded.

"I guess that's a good thing," Luke said. "At least

you have a kind of partnership going on now, and I'm hoping they'll keep an eye on you as well. This whole thing is unnerving."

"I know," she said. "I'm sorry we had to meet this way."

"I'm not," Luke replied. "If it weren't for Trini, you and I might never have crossed paths. I don't know what terrestrial or godly lineup made this union happen, but I can tell you that I'm grateful it did."

Catherine smiled and switched the phone into her left hand. "Are you saying you like me?" she teased.

"You know I do," he said. "The very first time I set eyes on you I whispered to myself that if I didn't see you with a husband or boyfriend, I was finding a way to meet my red-headed neighbor. You reeled me in first thing."

"Really? You noticed me from across the street?"

"Oh, yeah. I was keeping an eye out for your comings and goings, always glad to see you alone."

Catherine smiled. "My hair isn't red," she said. "It's auburn."

"In the sun, it's red, glorious red. I can't wait to get my hands on it again. I love your hair."

Catherine sat back in her chair and wished he was there with her.

"I suppose," he began, "that you're going out to cruise the strip again tonight."

"Yes," she said. "I could skip going but that might be the one time Trini would show her face. She's young. I'm not sure how long she'll stay in hiding. At some point, she just might get tired of staying invisible and I don't want to miss it."

"I understand," he said. "It's early September though, I'm a little concerned about what you're going to do when the summer crowd disperses. And shortly after your landlord will most likely want to drain the pipes in your cottage and seal things up. There's no heat in those places. I don't mean to be discouraging, Catherine, but I'm worried about how long you're going to stay and where."

Catherine took a deep breath. "I've thought of all that, too. But how do I just leave, Luke? I have no other leads on where my sister hung out."

Luke hesitated then said, "Honestly, she could be miles away. We wouldn't know if she left in the middle of the night."

"I know," she paused. "I think about that possibility every day. If Trini found a way to leave the area, there isn't anything I can do. I just feel her nearness, Luke. I don't know why, but it's the only hope I have." Catherine started to cry. "I want to know her, touch her; I want her to tell me about her childhood and I want to tell her about mine. I want to know her favorite color. I want to know her favorite foods, her favorite toy as a child. I want to hear about her first love. Luke, I need to find my sister."

"I know, Catherine. I'm sorry; I didn't mean to upset you."

"It's not you," she said. "It's the situation. You've made my summer bearable. I miss you so much. You've been my refuge."

"Don't think in past tense," he said. "I'm here for you, Catherine. If there's a time when you get some significant news, you call me. I'll be there no matter what I'm doing. I've already spoken to the college chancellor. He knows you're going through a stressful time and that I might need to take off suddenly. He's on board with us."

Catherine had been feeling immensely alone. Suddenly it seemed as if she had a support system. She put her hand over her mouth to conceal her sobs.

"Please," Luke said, "be very careful tonight, and call me when you get in, no matter what the time."

"I will," she promised.

Catherine sat in her rocking chair and stared at the dismal walls of the cottage. She thought about the families who, over the years, had occupied for a week or two, this very space. Most likely, they had left each morning for the beach and returned at the end of each day exhausted with joyful activity. It wouldn't matter if the cottage they rented was uninteresting and small – it was a place to rest after a day of fun. But now, the cottage was a little prison and a barely adequate shelter – there was no joy in being there.

The next day was Friday. A few stragglers came for the weekend, but the population had thinned over the past two weeks. Teachers and students headed back to school, vacation time was basically over. In general, Catherine found that the loss in numbers added to her loneliness. It was perplexing, but she supposed it was more to do with Trini's disappearance than throngs of people no longer roaming the strip.

Catherine made herself some tea and ate wedges of oranges; she thought she might have a slice of pizza in town later. She read for a while then took a shower and changed her clothes. The air was chilly; she wore jeans and a long-sleeved shirt as she locked her door and headed for the strip.

After walking for half an hour, Catherine walked into a pizzeria and ordered a slice with cheese and peppers. She bought a Coke to go along with it and sat at a counter to eat. It wasn't long before she attracted company, three or four men gathered around her asking what a beautiful woman like her was doing out on her own. She told each of them confidently that her boyfriend was working. She was getting good at fabricating, but when she thought of Luke, she realized that she wasn't so far from the truth.

With her meal finished, Catherine was glad to escape the eyes of the other patrons as she walked outside and noticed the strong scent of salt in the air. The tide, she assumed, was coming in and the feel of fall was definitely invading the night. With no heat in her cottage, Catherine wondered how long she would stay there. Perhaps she would need to splurge on a bed and breakfast; there was the possibility that the rates would be lower with the summer season fading. Elated with the idea of that change, she thought it might be interesting to live among other people, not isolated as in the cottage. Almost immediately after giving consideration to a bed and breakfast, Catherine thought about the complications that living in an occupied house might bring. She would stay put in the cottage for as long as she was allowed.

Her eyes sought the windows of closed shops. Most places were calling the season over with Labor Day in the past. As she took her eyes from a storefront filled with every color of shoes, Catherine again spotted the young man who had been living in the cottage next door. He was sauntering around by himself, looking grumpy. Aside from worrying about Trini's whereabouts, Catherine had not forgotten the young girl who had lived next to her. There was something pathetic about the girl's lack of energy and awareness. It was hard to distinguish between the problem of alcohol or drugs, but it seemed evident that one of those culprits was to blame for the girl's vulnerable condition. She wanted to walk up to the young man and ask him where the girl was and if she was well. She understood that she couldn't do that – it was none of her business.

Catherine sat down on one of the many benches scattered through town. She imagined that it had once been a place where the elderly enjoyed slow strolls and quiet afternoons. As the years passed, it gradually began being taken over by young motorcycle clubs, urging the elderly to find a more peaceful place in which to spend their summers.

Catherine thought about her childhood and teen vacations. They were always to other states, most often to the north. Those two weeks away meant not seeing her friends, leaving the family cat in the care of a neighbor Catherine didn't care for, and it meant packing and wearing clothing fit for high-end restaurants. Her parents were enthusiasts of multi-course meals where white linen tablecloths covered the tables and the waiters wore white jackets, white shirts, black slacks and black bowties. It was her parents' idea of relaxation, but it was boring to Catherine.

She thought about growing up among older

185

cousins, everyone around her was out of sync, too old to be interested in Catherine's world. She longed to grow up where she could have a life she would love with her own family, a pretty home, an abundance of creatures running around. Where had the dream gone? Was there still that possibility with Luke, or was he too good to be true? Life just seemed to happen. Riley had held her interest, although not enough to commit to marriage. She endured his death, and then she became a police officer. None of these things had been part of the plan.

Catherine's eyes scanned the fifteen to twenty people wandering the center of the street when her eyes stopped at someone who was staring at her. Not positive that it was she he was looking at, she turned her head just a bit to see if there was someone behind her. There was no one. She looked back at him, his eyes still fastened to hers and looking angry. It was the young man from the green cottage next door. His intensity sent a chill through Catherine's body as she stared back. The exchange was mystifying.

Catherine stood up. She didn't want to seem as if she was avoiding him, but she also didn't care to continue the staring match. As she started to walk, he moved closer to her, and then he stopped in the middle of the street and watched her walk. She had the urge to turn around to see if he was following her, but she didn't. When she had moved a few shops down, she looked at the reflection in the window and could see nothing of him. Catherine took a deep breath, turned around to face the street and found that her eyes could not locate him anywhere. She instinctively had not

186

liked him. She was certain that he had been cruel to the dark-haired girl sharing the cottage with him, but there was no proof, only intuition.

Catherine stopped at a café and ordered a hot coffee to go then she glanced once more at the sparsely traveled street and headed toward the cottage. Her steps were deliberate but slow. There was nothing and no one waiting for her except the bland walls and unmatched furniture. She hated the place and yet she felt compelled to stay.

Before inserting the key in the lock, she turned around and looked up and down the street. She could hear someone walking, their feet scuffing along on slightly sandy pavement. The person walked past. Catherine went into her cottage, locked the door and left her purse in a chair. As she placed her coffee on a small table, she dialed Luke's number.

"Hi," she said.

"Catherine. You're home a little earlier than usual, is everything all right?"

"Yeah," she said, not telling him about her former neighbor. "I'm just a little tired and there weren't a lot of people out on the strip. I decided to call it a night."

Luke audibly sighed. "Can't say it too often: I wish I was there or that you were here. Really, Catherine, I think it's going to get spookier and spookier the longer you're there and others start to disappear back into their normal lives. I wish you'd consider staying in a small hotel or something."

Catherine smiled. "Actually, that's a thought I had as well. If things become too weird, or the landlord here wants to close up, I'll stay in a b and b. Meanwhile, I'm okay. I'm bored out of my mind in this little place, and I'm admittedly lonely, but I'm okay. How are you?"

"Good. I like it here. This college is small and unpretentious, kind of like it was developed for kids who are smart but not in the groove. Do you know what I mean? It's not a party school, just expectations of decency. It's comfortable."

"It sounds like a good fit. I think part of me wishes it wasn't so, that you could come rushing back here to stay with me. But no, I'm actually glad that this is working out so well for you, Luke. I'm sure you're a good teacher."

"I try," he said. "I like the students; I tell them I'm accessible, and for the ones who seem shy, I prod a bit and sometimes they level with me about a difficulty they're having in their studies or in their lives. It's a pretty relaxed atmosphere. You'd like it here, I know you would."

Catherine hesitated before asking, "Do you miss the priesthood?"

Luke took his time replying. "Sometimes, yes."

Catherine's stomach tightened into a knot. "Would you ever go back?"

There was, she determined, more than one way to lose a man.

"No," Luke said. "I left when I felt sure that I was right. I needed to step out of the way and let someone completely devoted take my place. That's a position you need to feel deeply about. I wanted to, but it didn't happen. Teaching at a school like this is affirming day by day that I did the right thing. This is where I belong, at a little college where I can encourage and teach. I'm afraid I'll never be rich, Catherine."

"Do you think I care? I grew up in a family where every particle was budgeted. Vacations were factored in; I felt secure, I had what I needed. I'm good with that."

"Anything new on the street tonight?"

"Not really," she was slow to say.

"What does that mean? Explain please."

Catherine bit her lower lip and closed her eyes for a moment. "Oh, I just saw that character from next door, the young blond-haired guy who was with that poor girl."

"And?"

"And he kind of stared at me. It was pretty strange. I thought at first that he was looking at someone behind me – I was sitting on a bench in front of that shop where I bought my black dress. But, as it turned out, he was looking directly at me. Maybe he recognized me living next door – it was just a little unnerving."

"What happened? Did he end up speaking to you?"

"No, I started walking and when I turned to see if anyone was following me, I couldn't see him anywhere. He's really an angry looking young guy."

"I hate this," Luke said. "He knows exactly where you live."

"It's okay. I'm alert to anything unusual. Really, Luke, I'm okay."

"I wish you didn't need to reassure me quite so often," he said. "I'll be relieved when this is over. I don't want to seem insensitive about your sister. I want you to find her, but I also want you safe."

Catherine understood. She didn't envision herself

189

as a super hero in search of Trini. This was her mirror spirit, a sibling she had longed to be connected with, the imaginary friend she sought as a child. But she was aware of possible dangers. Trini knew the world of drugs and destruction. Catherine had been on the opposite end, trying to curb the problem as small as the increments might be. Catherine's hope was to find her sister, to ensure her good health and to destroy any addiction, even if it meant knowing her briefly before she would probably be sent back to Germany.

"Catherine, are you still there?"

"Yes," she said, half lost in her own thoughts.

"You sound weary."

"I'm just…I don't know what I am. I'm discouraged if nothing else. It's a little hard doing this alone. I knew my mom wouldn't be okay with this search. I don't blame her. Why would she want to know the illegitimate child my father had with another woman? She wouldn't, and neither would I in her place. But this would have been a lot easier to bear if I'd had a friend along for the ride. You know, someone to just unwind with. One of my friends was going to join me for a couple of weeks but she had to move away for her work. I think I'm just sick of myself," she laughed.

"I wish I could help," he said.

"You have. Without you, I'm not sure I'd still be here. I hope I would be; I'd like to think I had that determination on my own, but it's truly not fun. I'm more than grateful for the time you were here, and for this, for keeping in touch even though you're a distance away."

"And keep in mind what I told you. If something

comes up, I'll be there. No question."

Catherine could feel tears forming in her eyes and she was glad that Luke could not see them. "I think about that all the time, Luke. I can't tell you how much that means to me."

With their call ended, Catherine sat holding the phone and thought about what Luke had said. He wanted her to find Trini, but he didn't want to lose *her* in the process.

Catherine heard his concerns. She knew that if their positions were reversed, she would feel pure panic for his safety. He was in an impossible position, and perhaps more sympathetic than anyone else to her plight. Catherine accepted that her own mother would be more than slightly annoyed with this endeavor. She would suggest that Catherine leave it alone – let the girl go on her way. Support had come from one source, Luke Renoir.

Catherine took a quick shower, not thinking until she was drying her body that part of her reasoning for this urgency for cleanliness had something to do with the glaring eyes of her former neighbor. His stare at her had been penetrating, as if he was eerily conscious of Catherine's opinion of him and how he'd treated the young woman in his care. Of all the unsavory characters she'd come across in her search and in her former position with the police, this young man had made a very dark impression. There was something wrong with him.

Catherine decided to put him out of her thoughts as she changed into soft pajamas and climbed into bed. She pulled the sheet and a thin blanket up to her neck and lay in the dim light from the street lamp. It was quiet in the area now with so much less traffic and very few pedestrians walking by with their loud laughter. She wondered if she'd been fooling herself, thinking that this mission was going to end with a positive note. It had been suggested that maybe Trini had found a way to leave the area, but every time Catherine entertained that thought, she relied upon her own instincts – *Trini was near.*

Sleep came slowly that night as dreams invaded Catherine's rest. At one point she woke thinking that she'd heard a familiar sound. She listened for more but there was nothing. She thought about getting out of bed and looking at the empty cottage next door. The sound had seemed to come from there and now she hoped no one was breaking into the vacant space. Before she had made a decision to check, Catherine fell back to sleep, convincing herself that it had probably been the dream she'd had a few times before. It was the one of her father, home from work, closing his car door and smiling as he walked toward her when she was a little girl. Those had been precious memories, the ones before the break-up, the ones when Catherine's world was filled with security and not knowing that anyone, especially the people in her life, could be deceptive.

Chapter Thirteen

It was five in the morning when Catherine woke to hear birds chirping outside her window. She listened to the sweet conversation they seemed to be having with one another and thought about the more vocal gulls.

She walked in her bare feet to the kitchen and drew a glass of water from the faucet, then she thought about calling Luke. It was early, but if he wasn't already up, he'd need to be soon. She finished her water then dialed his number.

"Catherine, are you all right?" he asked with concern in his voice.

"I'm fine. I woke up earlier than usual and decided that misery likes company."

"If you're proud of yourself for waking me, sorry, I beat you to it. I was up watching the rabbits chomping on some salad I tossed out to them."

Catherine smiled. "Thousand Island or Raspberry Vinaigrette?"

"Excuse me?"

"Which do they prefer for a dressing?"

"Ah, so early in the morning you're playing tricks on me. They have plain old salad; just some greens. So, tell me what you're up to today."

Catherine sat down in her rocking chair and pushed her hair back from her face. "I have no specific plans.

I'm sure I'll meander through the beach area later, and I'll have coffee with the gulls in a few hours, but other than that, I'm feeling restless. I wish I had the slightest clue what to do next. I suppose I was naïve to think I'd just see Trini wandering around. Unless she has someone looking after her, I can't understand how she's remaining under cover. It's so frustrating."

"I can understand your disappointment. I was beginning to feel it myself before I came here. I hoped we'd spot her together."

Catherine's eyes went to the lace-covered window, the morning sun stealing slowly across the curtain and into the room.

"What time is your first class today?" she asked.

"Eight-twenty. I'm having coffee with Charlie at seven-thirty. He's asked me a couple of times if you've heard anything more regarding Trini. I know he would have liked to be helpful."

"He was. I liked learning about Trini, about the fact that she had twin brothers. I don't know if I ever would have found that out on my own. It never occurred to me that she could have siblings, other than me. It doesn't sound like she had the best relationship with them though. Maybe that's why she came here to be a nanny."

"I'm sure you two will have a lot to talk about someday."

"I hope so. But tell me more about Vermont. Have you been driving the back roads? I remember the gorgeous rolling hills and tons of stone walls."

"A lot of it is like that. It's beautiful. The college grounds are fairly flat and everywhere you look it's green. The grass is thick and healthy looking, which is probably why the rabbits like it so much. The trees are still a brilliant green and because they're mostly maples and oaks, there's an ample amount of shade everywhere. It's quite a contrast to our beach area so filled with sun. I'm anxious for you to see it."

Catherine smiled. "Sounds nice."

"You don't have any reservations about coming here, do you?"

Catherine shifted in her seat. "For a visit?"

"Well, yes, for a start. I mean, I fully intend to divide my time between the rocky shore of Rhode Island and here, but I'm hoping you're going to like this place as much as I do, for more than a visit."

Catherine swallowed and looked around at the room filling with light.

"Hey," he said, "are you there?"

"Yes, I'm here."

"Did I assume too much?"

"No," she said. "I'm just trying to get through today. Your description of the college grounds is so appealing, and I love that you want to spend time here with the gulls. Tell me about your house."

"It's brick with three bedrooms and a bathroom upstairs, which I don't use. Downstairs, there's a living room, dining room, kitchen, bathroom and office. I'm currently using the dining room for a bedroom."

"Was the house furnished?"

"Partially. The professor who lived here before me had much of his own things. He was sleeping in the dining room to avoid the stairs and he kindly left me a double bed, no mattress. I bought a new one and a few

195

other items. It's pretty sparse in here – I think I need you to come and advise me on what to buy."

Catherine sighed. It would be fun to help him choose some new items for the house. "I should let you go," she said. "It's six-thirty. I'll call you later tonight if you'd like."

"If you didn't call, I'd be frantic. Please be careful."

"I will," she said.

At ten, Catherine walked to town and bought bread for the gulls and a scone for herself. As usual, she went next door to buy coffee. About to turn around to leave the café, she almost collided with the detective she'd spoken to at the police station.

"Oops," he said good-naturedly, "nearly got that coffee of yours."

Catherine stopped. "Good morning," she said when she'd gained her composure.

"It does seem to be," he said with a slight smile and a nod. "Have you got a minute?"

"Is there something new concerning my sister?"

They walked toward a small round table and sat down. "I was going to ask you the same thing," he said. "By the way, did I introduce myself at our first meeting? I'm Jack Stearn."

Catherine smiled. "Yes, actually, you did. Great name for a detective."

"Yup, I've heard that before. So, anything new come your way?"

Catherine took a sip of her coffee then placed it down on the table. "Nothing. I search, I ask questions, I walk the town from end to end. I don't know what else to do."

Jack Stearn turned his paper cup around slowly, his eyes on Catherine. "Did you know her brothers are in town?"

Catherine could feel the surge of adrenalin in her chest. "Trini's brothers are here?"

Jack nodded. "Oh, yeah, I know those boys. The Bauer twins; they act normal, dress normal, but there's nothing normal about them. I watch them, I know they're up to something, but I'll be damned if I know what."

Catherine felt numb with that information. "Do you think they're hiding Trini?"

Jack Stearn looked around at the other patrons and then back at Catherine. "I wish I knew. I'm in the business of observation, but if I were to make a guess, I'd say they're after her more than protecting her."

Catherine's stomach went into knots. How awful that her sister's own brothers could be threatening, and why? Catherine leaned forward and whispered to Jack. "Could they be the two men who were after Trini? Could it be that straight forward – her brothers?"

Jack looked at Catherine's beautiful blue eyes. "I think so. They're a grim pair. When they first arrived here early in the summer, it was obvious they weren't here to collect some sun on their skin. There was a night when they were hauled into the station, a dispute developed over a girl. One twin took quite a beating in the altercation, but the other one came out unscathed. They don't smile. They are the most tight-lipped, serious young men I've ever come across."

"Do you know who the girl was? It wasn't Trini,

was it?"

"No," Jack said. "It was definitely not your sister."

Catherine took a sip of her coffee and shook her head. "It's perplexing. I don't get why they'd want to harm Trini. Part of me would like to meet them, to ask them what's going on, and part of me wants to beat them up."

Jack smiled. "Me too. My advice to you is that you keep your distance from them. I have people keeping an eye out for their antics, but so far there hasn't been anything I can drag them in for questioning on. They have this elusive quality, kind of like dark ghosts."

Detective Stearn and Catherine sipped their coffee then he stood. "I need to get going," he said, "but it was nice bumping into you."

"Thanks," she said. "It was nice to see you, too."

Catherine watched him walk out of the café and into the street; then she gathered her bread, scone and coffee as she prepared to walk back to the cottage. From there she would drive to the rocks and the gulls to share a late morning breakfast.

Every time she set foot on the smooth surface of the sea-washed boulders, Catherine thought about how much she missed Luke. No one had ever affected her so deeply. She was, without any doubt, completely in love with him. She had no hesitancy in admitting to herself, and *only* to herself, that Luke was the recipient of her concern and affections. Nothing he might do could turn her away from him.

She sat down on their rock and pulled a loaf of bread from a brown bag. The gulls stood at attention – they knew the routine. Catherine called to them as she tossed half slices into the air, watching as their graceful flight took them in precision movements to the airborne offerings. With their food delivered and them hoping for more, she nibbled on her scone and finished the last of her coffee. As Luke did, she gathered the paper goods together and sat on them so that they wouldn't blow out to sea. She placed sunglasses over her eyes and stared at the green-blue hues of swirling water licking at the rocks as the tide seemed to be backing away.

Catherine understood that her eyes were seeing a true wonder of the earth, but what had made the place magical was who she had experienced it with. She recalled seeing him for the first time all in black. His manner of moving, the sauntering glide to his steps; it was evident that he had a confidence about life. He knew what he was doing. He'd made important decisions and was secure in knowing that his conclusion was correct. Now she found it nothing short of magnificent to feel his concern, his love for her. She longed to hold his hand, to touch his strong shoulders, to lay with him bundled in bed covers, warm and fastened to his body.

That night walking in town brought nothing of any interest. Catherine walked into a café advertising hot cider and bought herself a cup before walking back to the cottage at ten-thirty. She would settle herself in and then she would call Luke.

Sitting in her pajamas and sipping the last of her now cooled cider, Catherine dialed Luke's number.

"I'm glad you're calling a little earlier tonight," he said.

"Why, were you hoping to head off to bed?"

"No, I just get anxious when evening comes. I know you're out there. Any particular reason you're early tonight?"

Catherine finished her cider and then leaned back in her chair. "It was quiet. The streets are getting less and less populated as the season ends. I thought the chances of spotting Trini in a thinned group were not good."

"You're probably right," he agreed.

"I did talk with the detective on the town's force though, Jack Stearn. He was at the coffee shop this morning. He told me something both interesting and disturbing."

"What's going on?"

Catherine shifted in her chair. "He told me that Trini's twin brothers are here."

"In town? They're at the beach?"

"Yes, they've been here all summer."

"What's that about?" Luke asked. "I don't like the sound of that, Catherine. Maybe they're the two men after your sister."

"Detective Stearn thinks that's a possibility. What we don't know is why. I was thinking about it this afternoon while I spent time on our rocks. If her brothers are the men looking for her, maybe she's not in the dire danger we thought. I mean, would brothers really do harm to their sister? Maybe they know she has a drug issue and they're trying to get her away from it all."

"Is that what the detective thinks?"

Catherine hesitated. "Well, no, he didn't say that.

He doesn't think much of the twins. Apparently they've been in a few scuffles this summer. He actually thinks they're sullen and troublesome. I don't know, Luke. I guess I'm trying to talk myself into believing that Trini is not in immediate danger. Maybe I'm kidding myself."

"You're wearing yourself down," Luke said softly. "I hate this. There's something sinister about those brothers. What are they doing there? There's no way they're protecting Trini. If they were, they'd walk into town with her and take care that no one harmed her. The fact that they're there at the beach is troubling. I don't like it."

Catherine closed her eyes for a moment and sighed.

"I don't mean to sound so negative," he said. "I'm sorry, Sweetheart."

Catherine smiled, she liked the sound of *Sweetheart*. "I know," she said, "I understand. Tell me what you did today. Did you have coffee with your friend?"

"Yes, Charlie and I had a good visit in the cafeteria. His wife is a nurse in the local clinic. She left for work at five this morning so he was ready for a hearty breakfast. He's a good guy, a walking encyclopedia."

Catherine smiled. "Your age?"

"No, he's got few years on me I think. He's been part of the faculty here for thirty years."

"Holy smoke," she said. "He must be close to sixty. So, after breakfast with Charlie, you had classes all day?"

"Most of the day. I have a free hour and a half in the middle of the day. Sometimes I use that time to correct papers, other times I take a nice walk. Today I walked. It's really beautiful here, Catherine. You're going to love it."

Catherine laughed. "I love the way you assume I'm going up there."

Luke was quiet for a moment. "I can hope."

"Do more than hope," she said.

"Count on it," he said.

"So, are you still coming down next weekend?"

"There isn't a thing in the world that would stop me. Yes. I'll be there."

Catherine rocked in her chair and smiled. "I can't wait."

"Me too. I've already booked us a room, the same one at that nice little hotel by the sea."

Catherine felt a chill. "I liked that place."

"I liked *you*," he said.

Catherine hugged her own arms. She thought about Luke being her heaven, and then she almost laughed thinking about the irony given his former vocation.

"How are our gulls doing?" he asked.

"They're fine. They've inquired about you actually. I told them you'd pay them a visit soon. They're feeling abandoned."

"Go ahead," he said, "make me feel guilty."

Catherine laughed. "The gulls and I understand."

"I'll get them an extra loaf of bread when I visit."

"And what will you give to me?" she asked with a flirty tone in her voice.

Luke laughed. "How did I end up with such a

naughty girl?"

"Just lucky, I guess," Catherine said with a smile.

They spoke for a few more minutes and when the call ended Catherine sat in her chair and held the phone to her lips.

It was just before midnight when she decided to go to her bed and try for some sleep. Her room was dark and when she went by the window, the cottage next door was in shadows. Streaks of golden light from the street lamp dared to touch the small structure, but not enough to make its exterior plainly visible. Catherine looked at the place and felt that same sense of loneliness for the girl who had lived there. She wanted to believe that the girl was well, that perhaps she went off to college. Catherine knew that the reality of that was not entirely valid. Girls like her were often on route to a tough and short life.

Catherine pulled the covers to the side and climbed in between the sheets. She thought about Luke; he was an incredible find. Having known and cared for Riley, she had believed that sharing a life with someone was probably out of the question. She needed to trust, and Riley, as sweet, handsome and charming as he was, did not seem capable of being exclusive. That wasn't going to work for Catherine. She wasn't sure why, but with Luke everything felt different.

Catherine thought about Detective Stearn. She liked him. He reminded her of her father who had spent twenty-eight years on the police force, happy to walk his beat as he protected the small community where they lived. She wondered if Detective Stearn had a family. Close to her father's age, she hoped that this man was someone who went home at night to a comfortable environment.

Before she closed her eyes, Catherine looked through the window to the dark sky. She thought about how different life could be with Trini at her side. All that had once been a unit, her parents, her friends, Riley, were absent. Having a sister to talk with, to go shopping with, to spend birthdays with, would make a positive difference. The present existence, Catherine decided, was incredibly lonely. As she turned onto her side, she thought about Luke. She wished he was there, next to her. Through this trying summer, he had been a Godsend.

When she closed her eyes, she thought how silent it was. She was accustomed to hearing people walking past her cottage until the early hours of morning. Now it was still. She turned onto her back and opened her eyes to the shadowy gray ceiling. She closed her eyes again and then was startled by what sounded like a trashcan being tipped over outside. Convinced that it was the work of raccoons, she lay quietly, listening for more. Several minutes passed before Catherine sat up in bed and placed her bare feet on the floor. It was more than a raccoon. She reached for her cell phone and held it while she waited, alert to more sounds. It was distinctly footsteps she heard now, on dry grass and gravel.

Catherine held her breath as she slid off the bed and to her knees. There, she moved toward the window but saw nothing. She stood then crouched down as she went into her front room and toward the lace covered glass. Her eyes struggled to scrutinize any movement in the street, but she saw nothing. The sounds were gone. No footsteps. Since the cottages on each side of hers were empty, the place had an eerie feeling. Catherine walked to her rocking chair and sat down, clutching the phone to her chest.

Calming her breathing, Catherine reasoned that perhaps it was someone who'd had one too many. No one would purposely knock over a trashcan in the middle of the night unless they were stone drunk.

After more than an hour of listening for every scant sound, Catherine pulled her bare feet up onto the chair's seat. She hugged her knees and closed her eyes, drifting into a light sleep. When the dim light of morning crept through the window and touched the pink and green floral pattern on the sofa, Catherine blinked and felt glad for the light.

She changed into jeans and a shirt before heading into town for coffee. She would pick up the bread and another coffee later, closer to eleven when the gulls were accustomed to having their treats.

Catherine found the beach strip quiet at seven in the morning. A few people carried canvas bags and summoned little children who sleepily tagged behind as they headed for the sandy shore. Most people, Catherine thought, were probably still asleep, having stayed up late socializing.

She walked into the café where the coffee was best and nearly bumped into Jack Stearn.

"You're an early bird," he said to her with a smile.

"I am," she said. "I always feel like I'm missing something if I don't get up with the sun. I usually make myself an early morning cup of tea, but today I felt the urge for coffee."

Jack smiled as he gestured toward a small table. "If you're getting coffee, I'll wait here for you if you don't mind."

"That would be great," she said. Within a few moments, Catherine was back and sat down to join the detective.

"How are things going," he asked. "Anything new?"

"I wish there was. No, I keep looking, and I'll continue for as long as I can, but it's discouraging. If my sister was injured or sick, I would have no way to know. When I first arrived here, I called the local clinic. They don't want to divulge anything, so it's hard. I keep hoping that somehow I'm going to know that she's okay. At this point, that would be enough. I had such high hopes of seeing her, meeting her, getting to know her. Part of *me* is missing."

Jack Stearn nodded. "I understand. Well, the only thing I can tell you is that she has not left the country. She's over-stayed her time here; she was scheduled to return to Germany a few months ago. I'm sure that's a consideration of hers, that the authorities, as well as the two men, are looking for her. I still think there's every possibility that those guys are her brothers."

Catherine swallowed a sip of coffee. "I wish I knew why."

Jack shook his head. "This mile long strip of beach draws in some pretty strange individuals. Not to say all of them are strange, many are people who don't have a lot of money and this is their idea of a vacation. But it definitely brings in some dark types. Lots of chances to

206

deal in drugs, both buying and selling; it keeps us on our toes. That's what made your sister stand out to the force. She's been here before. She was this fresh-faced kid who looked healthy and happy. She didn't look the part."

"Did you ever speak to her?" Catherine asked.

Jack shook his head. "No. I may have nodded to her or said hi, but I never had a conversation with her. The kids around here can smell a cop a mile away – they don't want to talk to us. We leave them alone as long as they behave themselves." Jack winked at Catherine. "I was young once, too."

Catherine returned the smile. "Some of the young officers in my hometown could be a bit wild. I found it amusing that so many of them had been, in one way or another, bad boys or troublesome girls. I had a friend in college who was a minister's son. He rode a motorcycle, wore black leather everything, and out-ran state troopers by dashing through fields on his cycle. It makes you wonder if some people retaliate by being the opposite of their disciplined parents' rules and regulations. The odd thing is that college friend is now a minister himself."

Jack smiled. "Well, I suppose experience helps."

They each sipped their coffee, their eyes on patrons ordering their first cup of the day or breakfast.

"Did you by any chance hear anything out of the ordinary last night, way into the morning hours?"

Catherine hesitated. "I heard a loud clanking of what sounded like a trash can. I thought it might be raccoons, I know they hang out around the cottages. I think I heard footsteps. Nothing more than that, but why, did something happen up my way?"

"One of our infamous twins apparently had a little too much joy juice and he went stumbling around up your way. He woke a couple about three cottages down from you and they called us. When we found him, he was being sick by the dunes. We took him in to protect him more than anything, but he's off and running as of six this morning. He's not exactly a conversationalist. He looks through you, if you know what I mean. Not a lot of personality going on there."

Catherine shivered. "Strange," she said, "that Trini's brother was up wandering around my place. I don't know why, but I have this kind of subconscious attitude about the twins. I don't think, even though they're related to my sister, that I would like them."

Jack nodded. "I can tell you that they don't resemble your sister at all. They don't look like her and they are plain sullen. Your sister has a youthful glow. The twins look like they've been through a war and lost. So," he said, "what's your day entail?"

Catherine shrugged one slim shoulder. "I'm becoming a creature of habit. I go every day around eleven to the rocks along the northern shore. I have coffee with the gulls while they eagerly consume a loaf or two of bread. Evenings, I walk the strip, mingle with people at cafés and bars, I show Trini's photo to some. I'm trying hard to be subtle; I don't want to scare people away who could say something useful, but I am desperate to find the slightest clue to her whereabouts."

"Has anyone given you anything positive?"

Catherine shook her head. "Not really. One shopkeeper indicated seeing Trini early in the season.

Another girl, a waitress in a café, obviously recognized Trini when I showed her the photo. She walked away from me. I think she might have known Trini, but I couldn't get a word out of her."

Jack Stearn nodded. "That's the attitude we get on the force every day. Sometimes I'd like to shake them, but then *we'd* be behind bars." Jack stood and placed his empty cup in the trash. "This has been a pleasant visit. If you need us, you know where to find us," he said.

Catherine thanked him and watched as he left the café. She ordered another coffee to go, went to the bakery for bread then walked back to her cottage. Without going inside, she opened her car door, slipped behind the wheel, started the engine and drove to the rocks. She would call Luke once she was there, just to check in and to let him hear the shrill of the gulls.

Chapter Fourteen

Friday night at nine-thirty, as she slipped into a light jacket for her beach strip stroll, Catherine heard a knock at the door. The noise stopped her. She listened for another knock and it came. She edged closer to the door, her right ear against the flat surface.

"Catherine," he said.

Her heart danced with joy. She hadn't expected Luke until morning, but there he was. She quickly unlocked the door and slid the bolt to the side. Luke turned the knob and walked in. Catherine reached up to put her arms around his neck, to hug him close.

Luke's arms tightened around her, his lips moved on her neck, then to her mouth.

"Oh, my God, I'm so glad to see you," she said softly. "I thought you were arriving in the morning."

"So is this an inconvenient time for you?" he teased as he pulled away enough to smile and let her see it.

She moved close enough to him to feel his heartbeat, to feel the warmth of his skin through their clothes.

"I thought I'd get here in time to walk the strip with you, and then we can check into our room."

Catherine looked up at him. "This is the best surprise ever."

Luke placed his large hands at the sides of her face and drew her close, kissing her firmly on her willing lips. "I have missed you," he said.

Catherine smiled as she tightened her grasp to his waist. "Would you like a cold drink before we go? I have Cokes and bottled water."

"Let's get something in town," he suggested as he opened the door. They stepped outside, locked the door then turned toward the beach strip. As they drew closer to the cafés and shops, Luke moved his grasp from around her waist to holding her hand. "Boy, it's gotten quiet here, hasn't it? Looks to me like about eighty percent of the population has gone."

"That's true," Catherine said. "In some ways it makes the search easier, not so many faces to scan, but it also makes it more difficult. I would think that with less people around, Trini might be more afraid to come out."

Luke nodded. "I think you're right. Come on," he said as he maneuvered Catherine into a café and lounge. "Let's have a drink – maybe a glass of wine?"

"Pinot Grigio with ice, yes," Catherine said.

They chose a dimly lit booth where they could see the street and the few passers-by.

"I can't believe you're here," she said as she looked across the table at him. "It's been a long couple of weeks."

Luke reached across for her hands. "For me too. Before I met you, I never could have said this, but I'm actually glad to be back here. It feels good to be with you on this mission. And tomorrow feeding our feathered friends will be fun."

211

With their wine, they shared a small sampler of cheese, crackers and fruit, then walked for more than two hours along the beach strip. The air had turned cool and crisp and the scent of salt surrounded them. Gone were the permeating odors of stale beer and onion rings.

"I think," Catherine said as they stopped to look in a boutique window, "that I am tired. And you must be also. What time did you leave Vermont to get here at nine-thirty?"

"About four. If it hadn't been for Friday traffic on the highway, I'd have been here earlier. I thought about stopping for coffee, but decided against it – couldn't wait to get here."

Catherine wrapped her arm around his waist and smiled up at his handsome face. "Are we ready to go?"

With a look of devotion and desire on his face, Luke leaned in to her and kissed her lips. "I'm ready."

They walked hand in hand back to the cottage where Catherine slipped a nightgown, slippers and a change of clothes into a small overnight bag. In Luke's car, they drove a short distance to the small hotel where they'd stayed before.

"This is *our* room," Catherine said as she walked in toward the French doors with a view to the sea. "Nice work," she said as she turned around to face him.

"Thank you," he replied as he walked toward her, his hands pulling her to him.

"Now what?" Catherine asked playfully.

"Well, since you asked," Luke began, "I thought we'd play a little cop and robber."

Catherine laughed. "Oh, really?"

Luke looked at her in a flirty and threatening way.

"Yup, only this time, the robber wins."

Catherine felt her heart beat faster than she realized it could. She moved from the French doors and walked a few feet away from Luke.

"Scared?" he asked.

"Why," she asked, "are you going to give me penance?"

With that remark, Luke took two strides until he was before her, lifting her high into the air before planting her on the wide bed. "I think you're going to be sorry for that remark," he said as he pinned her to the mattress with his body and claimed her mouth with his.

One article of clothing after the other was discarded until the only thing between them was heat. They happily exhausted themselves then slept. With morning, they found one another again then shared a shower before breakfast.

"It's nearly eleven," Luke said consulting his watch as they finished scrambled eggs and fruit. "How about if we pick up the bread and coffee in town then head for the rocks?"

Catherine nodded and stood. "Sure, let's do that," she said smiling at her handsome companion.

On the rocks together, Catherine thought she could not possibly feel more for a human being than she did for Luke. She watched him, the pure joy on his face as he tossed bread to the gulls; his eyes fastened on the majestic sea. It was amazing to her that the two of them had existed for so many years without one another. If she had ever known at any time in her lonely life that she would meet Luke Renoir, she could have been more

213

joyful – the wait would have been worth it.

He looked at her and said, "They're looking well fed. Not a skinny one in the flock."

Catherine sipped her coffee and smiled. "What kind of a seagull mother would I make if I hadn't fed our little pals?"

Luke looked at her and then reached for her hand. "I cannot believe I found you," he said.

Catherine looked at him and before tears would flow, she looked away with a squeeze to his hand.

"What else would you like to do today?" he asked. "I know we'll check out the strip this evening, but we have several hours to do something fun. What will it be?"

"I'd love to go to the city mall," she said. "It's not like I'm a champion shopper or anything, but I love being by the river there and I love the cheerfulness of the place. I did try to go once, but without you, I just couldn't do it."

"Good," he said as he stood pulling her up to him. "Let's go. We'll be back here tomorrow, guys," he shouted to the gulls. Collecting their coffee cups, they made their way along the rocks to the street and the parking area, empty except for Luke's car.

The drive toward Providence was scattered with light conversation and periods of silence; they were once again content to be near one another. Walking along the river for an hour, Catherine looped her left arm into Luke's right. She thought about how she'd never felt so possessed and possessive before. She might very well be willing to concede her independence to share Luke's life.

214

"I'm starving," Luke said as he stopped walking and looked at Catherine. "Would you be ready for something to eat? There are some great restaurants here, unless you were counting on eating in the mall."

"I'm hungry, too. How about if we eat over there?" She pointed to a glass-front restaurant on the river's edge.

"Looks perfect," he said as he led her across a bridge and to their destination. They enjoyed a glass of wine with their meal then walked back to the mall. Inside they meandered through the varying levels like a pair of teenagers infatuated with one another. Luke bought himself a pair of shoes and Catherine bought a silk scarf to send as a Christmas gift to her mother.

When Luke decided to look at shirts in a men's clothing store, Catherine went next door to a unique gift shop. They met back in the hallway of the festive mall with new packages in their hands.

"I have loved this day," she said when they were driving back toward the beach.

"And I love you," Luke said with a quick glance at her. Her smile was subtle as she looked away. She wanted to tell him how she felt – she needed to find that strength within her – he deserved it.

That night in their hotel room, Catherine and Luke changed into jeans and light jackets then drove to her cottage before they walked the strip, each of them carrying cups of hot coffee. The area was eerily quiet, as if everyone had gone to sleep. For one brief moment, Catherine's heart raced as she caught a glimpse of a blonde-haired girl walking out of a café. The girl turned and Catherine could see that there was no resemblance

215

to Trini.

"I think," she said at eleven-thirty, "that we should stop for tonight. Half or more of this town is closed between the end of the season and the hour. Let's go."

"Are you sure?" Luke asked.

Catherine nodded and Luke squeezed her hand. They walked back to Catherine's cottage where she folded fresh clothing into a small overnight case. Alone in her bathroom, she took a quick look at her legs and ran her hands from knees to ankles. They were smooth. She smiled as she reached for a small bottle of almond oil and placed a touch of it at her throat and more behind her ears.

"Ready?" Luke asked as she emerged from her room.

"Ready," she said as they walked out toward Luke's car then drove to the secluded hotel by the sea.

"I have something for you," he said with his hands fastened at her back, his lips moving over the softness of her neck.

Catherine brushed her lips across his and then arched her back enough to look into his beautiful eyes. "You do? Well I have something for you, too."

They laughed teasingly and then Luke released her gently as he moved toward the bag from the men's shop. He opened it and pulled out a bundle of white tissue and then a long-sleeved pale blue shirt. He unfolded it to show its length and held it up to her.

"What's this?" she asked with a smile.

"Your night wear," he said.

"Oh, really?"

Luke smiled and stuffed his hands into his trouser

pockets. "I've always thought it would be devilishly interesting to be with a girl in a man's shirt – *only* a man's shirt."

"I see," she said as she accepted the shirt and held it against her. "And should I be overwhelmed with surprise that you've entertained such thoughts prior or during your former vocation?"

Luke pursed his lips and squinted at her. "I had my dreams."

Catherine moved close to him and kissed him lightly. "I guess we'll have to see if I can fulfill those dreams tonight."

Luke smiled. "I have no doubts."

Catherine left the shirt on the bed and then walked toward where she'd left her purse and a small package. She turned and walked to Luke, the package extended to him. "This," she said, "is for you."

Luke took the package and sat down on the edge of the bed. He was both surprised and delighted to unwrap a ten-inch tube of copper with a glass piece at one end. He looked at it and then in it. "This is beautiful," he said. "I've never owned a kaleidoscope."

Catherine sat down next to him as he held it to the light, the myriad of glass fragments dancing around as he turned the piece with a circular motion.

"I wanted you to have an idea of what it was like to experience synesthesia. Seeing the shapes and colors together in this magical little tube offers you at least a hint of what I see and love."

Luke looked at her as if she was the magic in his life and then he leaned toward her and kissed her lips. "You're amazing," he whispered. "Thank you."

217

As morning light filtered through the sheer curtains in the pretty room, Catherine lay in Luke's arms, her pale shirt open at the throat. He looked at her, her hair in disarray, her blue eyes glimmering with soft light and sleepiness; he smiled as he kissed her forehead. "Are you hungry?" he asked.

Catherine squirmed closer to him and nodded. "A little bit. I think I want waffles swimming in maple syrup. We could do just coffee with the gulls later."

"Sounds perfect," he said.

They lay in the quiet of early day, content with being close, neither of them wanting to move.

"I think," Catherine said, "that we should always come here, to this hotel, to this very room, when we want a get-a-way."

Luke hugged her gently. "I couldn't agree more," he said as he leaned up on his left elbow and then over her for a long, caressing kiss. When he had thoroughly devoured every angle of her parted lips, he pulled away and looked at her. "Waffles?" he said.

Catherine nodded. "But first, a shower." She swung her bare legs to the side and slid out of bed then turned and looked at him. "Are you coming?" she asked with a little smile.

It didn't take more than a split second for Luke to be out of bed, ready to join her in the glass enclosure.

With damp hair and folding her shirt across the bed as she dressed for breakfast, Catherine smiled as she noticed Luke with the kaleidoscope aimed at the window's light.

"I think we chose wonderful gifts for one another," she said, "but maybe we should have kept them for

Christmas; it's not so far off."

"We'll have one another for Christmas," he said as he placed the copper tube down and walked to her, wrapping his arms around her waist.

"So you'll be my gift and I'll be yours?" Catherine asked seductively.

"Yes. And there's an old French sentiment that makes the claim that whatever is given at Christmas, can never be taken back. You'll be mine. I'll be yours, forever."

Catherine smiled. "Did you make that up?"

Luke kissed her neck and then smiled at her. "Yes, but that's the way it's going to be."

Catherine pulled him so close to her that she wondered where she began and ended – her body against his was all she needed. She was giving in.

After rocking her gently back and forth, Luke kissed her lightly. They finished dressing and made their way to the quiet dining area where they seated themselves at a table with a superb ocean view.

"I never get tired of this," Luke said. "The ocean is so dependable."

Catherine nodded. "I never thought of it that way, but you're right. I think that's why I found myself drawn to the rocks where we feed the gulls. It's sedating. It puts you and your worries in place and you begin to understand that we're all these tiny, complicated particles on earth. Yes, we have troubles and concerns, but who doesn't?"

A waiter brought them steaming coffee and left them with menus.

Luke took a sip of coffee then focused on

Catherine. "One of the truths I learned as a priest is that as you said, we all have issues to endure. No one's pain is too small to consider. One person might be losing a child while another is losing a parakeet. The pain is there, as important and terrible for one as the other."

The waiter returned and took their orders for breakfast. When he had moved on to another table, Catherine looked at Luke and wondered how she had been lucky enough to have met him. He was a rare breed – sweet, caring, and handsome. She had him for one more day and she was going to make the most of it.

"When we leave here, are we going to town for bread?"

"We will. We'll have a nice visit with the gulls and then what would you like to do with the rest of the day?"

"Well, what time do we have to check out?"

"I have booked the room through tonight."

Catherine leaned back in her chair when the waiter arrived with their food and fresh coffee.

"I'm not sure," she said. "Our favorite places are here, on the rocks, and at the mall. As long as I have you at my side, I'll be happy," she said almost choking back tears.

Luke looked at her as he raised his coffee cup to his lips and then set the cup back on its saucer. "Watch it," he said. "I'm going to get the idea that you like me."

Catherine swallowed. She knew that she should have taken that moment to tell him the truth — she was completely in love with him. Instead, she smiled shyly and looked down at the unfinished waffles. She forced herself to eat another few bites to avoid speaking. They finished their coffee and walked back to their room.

"I suppose we can just leave our things as they are," she said as they pulled the bed covers neatly in place and hung clothing in the small closet.

"I think that would be fine," Luke said as he reached for her hand. "Come on, let's go feed our kids."

Luke and Catherine drove to town and pulled up to the café where they had been buying their morning coffee all summer.

"Would you like to come in with me?" he asked as he unfastened his seat belt and smiled at Catherine.

"I think I will. And then we can walk to the bakery for the bread."

Luke opened his door, walked to Catherine's side of the car and, as she opened the door, he took her hand. They walked into the café, ordered their coffee then Catherine felt a tap on her shoulder.

"Good morning," Detective Stearn said to her and then he nodded to Luke. Catherine made the introductions and the men shook hands.

"Have you got a minute?" Jack Stearn asked Catherine.

Catherine looked at Luke, asked if he was okay with that, and then the three of them sat down at a round table by the window.

"Anything new about your sister?" Jack asked after taking a swallow of his coffee.

Catherine shook her head. "Absolutely nothing," she said.

Jack nodded. "Did you hear all the commotion around here last night?"

Catherine glanced at Luke then back at Jack. "We were walking in town until after eleven. It was pretty quiet. What happened?"

Jack looked into Catherine's beautiful eyes and then he looked at Luke before he spoke. "You didn't hear anything around two in the morning?"

Catherine and Luke looked at each other briefly. "We actually weren't in the immediate area," she said, blushing slightly.

Jack looked out to the street and then back at Catherine. "There was an incident," he said. "A shooting."

"What?" Catherine said with fright in her voice. "What happened? Was anyone injured?"

Jack swallowed more coffee then nodded. "Someone died."

Catherine's right hand flew over her mouth. "Oh, my God, please don't tell me it was my sister."

"No, no," he assured her quickly. When he noted that Catherine's breathing had returned to normal, he looked at Luke and then to Catherine. "The victim was one of the twins," he said softly.

Catherine placed her cup down and sat motionless, her eyes on Jack.

"One of Trini's brothers?" Luke asked.

Jack nodded. "Yes."

Catherine's head pounded with questions. "How?" she asked. "What happened? Who did the shooting?"

"I can't talk too much about the case," Jack said. "I shouldn't be talking about it at all, but I think these are mitigating circumstances. The twins had an issue with someone who showed up in town a few days ago. The altercation took place and Hans Bauer was killed."

Catherine felt that her mouth had been filled with cotton. She shook her head. "And the other twin?"

"Eric. He's in custody. He'll go through the legal system and ultimately be deported. He wasn't here legally; neither of them were."

Catherine looked at Luke and then back at Jack. "Did anything surface about Trini?"

The detective shook his head. "I'm sorry," he said.

All three were quiet for several minutes when Luke spoke. "I wonder if this could mean that we'd now have a better chance of spotting Trini. If she no longer has them to fear, maybe she'd come out of hiding."

"Trouble is," Jack said, "it might not have been just the twins who were looking for her. We can hope, but we can't count on it."

Catherine sat back in her chair and stared at her coffee cup.

"There's more," Jack Stearn said.

Catherine and Luke looked at him.

"For most of the summer, the Bauer twins lived in the green cottage next to yours."

Catherine could feel the adrenalin race through her body. "Oh, my God. That accounts for me feeling confused over the constant change of clothes. I thought it was one man who changed his outfits – going out in blue and returning in brown. I never gave a thought to the idea of twins. Right next to me? That's incredible. How crazy is that?"

Jack nodded. "I need to go," he said as he stood, "but if I hear more, or you just want to check in with me, I'll tell you what I can. Meanwhile, we'll all keep our eyes out for your sister."

Catherine was silent. Luke stood and shook hands with the detective then sat back down and took Catherine's hand.

"I need to get out of here," she barely whispered.

Luke took her to the car, went to buy bread, then returned to the car where Catherine sat staring straight ahead.

Without a word Luke fastened his seat belt, started the engine and drove to the rocky shore where the gulls waited.

Catherine moved over the rocks as if in a trance, but once at their destination, she sat down and seemed quelled by the sea and its surroundings. With a few slices of bread in her hands, she tore tiny pieces and tossed them not far from where she sat. Luke sailed whole slices into the air, watching the gulls dip and glide for their food, his eyes going to Catherine every few seconds. With the bread devoured, Catherine sat quietly next to Luke for more than an hour. It was inconceivable for her to think of the twins living in close proximity. Had they known who she was? Could they possibly have thought that Catherine might attract Trini and draw her out of hiding? What could they possibly have wanted with their sister?

"Hey," Luke said as he covered her hand with his own. "Are you okay?"

Catherine moved her eyes from the sea to Luke. "I feel a little numb. I don't know what to think of the twins living right next to me all this time and I had no idea."

"How could you know?" Luke asked softly. "I'm

sure it was a strange coincidence, Sweetheart, but I can imagine how perplexing it must seem to you. They never acted like they were even aware of you, did they?"

"No. They were distinctly unfriendly. God, Luke, I could never have guessed that there were two of them. I thought it was one young guy who changed his clothes more often than anyone I'd known. And I can't help wondering what it was that they wanted from Trini. There are so many unanswered questions. I wish I could speak to Eric. I wish I could ask him about Trini, why he and his twin wanted to find her."

Luke moved closer to Catherine and wrapped his long arms around her.

"I'm not in any way diminishing your concerns about Trini, but I will be so happy to take you away from here. Not forever, I know we'll return often, we love this place. But I know you'll love Vermont. Just as the sea is soothing here, the hills are calming there. And you'll have me," he said with a gentle hug.

Catherine looked at his handsome face and smiled as she leaned toward him for a kiss. "I hope," she said, "that we'll have the coming holidays together."

"Oh, we will," Luke said, "there's no question about that. In fact, I think we should plan for a very special Christmas Eve."

Catherine gave him a quizzical look. "What do you have in mind?"

Luke rested his chin against her left shoulder. "I was thinking you in a white dress – me in a dark suit – a few close friends and a wedding cake."

Catherine looked at him with tears in her eyes.

225

"Really?"

"Oh yah," he said, "really."

Catherine sniffed and then swept tears away. "Aren't you supposed to *ask* me to marry you?"

"Are you kidding, and give you the chance to delay or say no?"

Catherine closed her eyes and leaned against him. "I'm going to hate when you leave," she said.

"I know," he replied with his lips pressed against her hair, "me too."

They sat close for several minutes before Luke felt Catherine shiver. "Are you cold?" he asked.

"Maybe. I think part of it is that I feel a little traumatized. Getting hard news can have that effect on people, making them feel cold, compromised."

"Would you like to go back to our room where we could order some hot coffee and relax? I'm sure you're still going to want to go to the beach strip this evening. A little rest might be good."

"Yes," she said. "Let's do that."

Luke stood and reached down for her hands, pulling her to her feet. They walked to his car and drove to the hotel. There, Catherine discarded her light jacket and sat down on the bed, then leaned back against the pillows. Luke ordered coffee and sandwiches then sat next to her until the food arrived.

"Come on," he said to her, "have a sandwich. You need to keep energized."

Catherine propped herself up on one elbow. She ate a small, triangular-shaped sandwich on toast and drank some coffee; then she lay back against the pillows and slept, Luke at her side.

Chapter Fifteen

It was hours later with the sun resting against the glimmering horizon when Luke and Catherine woke. She looked at the tinge of peach color in the sky and Luke looked at her blue eyes.

"What time is it?" she asked sleepily.

Luke looked at his watch. "Nearly seven; I can't believe we slept for so long. We should think about dinner and then we can go into town."

Catherine nodded and swung her legs out of bed placing her bare feet on the carpet. She stood and walked to the window, her eyes to the ocean. Luke joined her, his large, reassuring hands on her shoulders, his face next to hers. "Feel better?" he asked.

Catherine shrugged lightly. "I'm not tired, but I still feel overwhelmed with the news about the twins and the worry for Trini's safety. I'm scared to death, Luke. I've been getting more and more attached to the idea of having a sister – I've imagined what it would be like to know her. I understand that we're very different, but my dad's blood runs in our veins. That must count for something."

"Of course it does," he said. He stroked her hair gently and then placed his hands at her waist. "Let's get ready for dinner. We'll relax and then head out to walk the strip."

"I don't know if I can eat."

Luke looked at her for a moment then said, "You need to, Catherine. I don't care what you eat or how much, but please have something. You'll feel better, I promise."

Catherine chose a house salad and a cup of chowder. Luke decided on the same. When they'd finished their meals and watched the sun disappear, they drove to Catherine's cottage where they intended to park the car while they walked. Luke started to shut off the engine when Catherine begged him not to.

"I can't stand being here," she said. "I don't know how I can possibly remain in this cottage knowing that those horrible twins were living next to me. And it was them with that poor girl. Luke, please stay with me while I pack up my things and leave here."

"No problem," he said. "How about if we walk the strip for a while, then we can come back here and collect your belongings. You can stay at our hotel room."

Catherine shook her head. "I can stay there for a few days, but I can't really afford to stay there for long. I'll find a bed and breakfast or something."

Luke maneuvered the car out into the street and toward town. He parallel parked at a pizza shop and from there they walked to the familiar area where young inhabitants tended to spend their time. It was a Sunday night. The activity was slow, but still people wandered about laughing, drinking, smoking, some holding hands.

Catherine watched carefully for anyone who might have disguised themselves. If Trini's brothers were no longer a threat, would the girl dare to catch a breath of fresh air and freedom? That thought gave Catherine new hope.

"Would you like to have a coffee or another warm drink as we walk?" Luke asked.

Catherine nodded. "Yes, that would be nice."

They stopped long enough to step into their favorite coffee shop then continued to stroll through the streets, pausing to look in windows, always on the alert.

"When will you need to leave?" Catherine asked.

"I'll stay with you for a while tonight," he said as he lightly squeezed her hand. "I'll head out early, maybe around four. My first class isn't until nine-fifteen."

"Isn't that cutting it close? I don't want you to drive fast and tired. If it would be better for you to go tonight, please Luke, go. I need you to stay safe."

He squeezed her hand again and then draped his arm around her waist. "I'll be fine leaving at four. I'll call you when I get near to the college so you won't have to worry."

Catherine said nothing. She would worry, and she would miss him terribly.

"Tell me more about your house," she said. "I want to picture you there."

Luke smiled. "It's brick with white trim. All the faculty houses are similar, but each has an ample yard and lots of privacy. My house has bedrooms upstairs I don't currently use, and downstairs, well, you'd love the kitchen. It has a thick plank of pine for a center island. There are scratches and scars on the wood from use, but it has this warm patina. The view from the

229

kitchen window is of maples, oaks and rabbits. It's great, you'll see." Luke hesitated and Catherine was quiet. "There's also a decent deck off the back of the house through a French door in the kitchen. The fellow who had the house before me left a small barbeque grill. It looks pretty corroded; I'm going to buy another. I'll be able to cook you a mean hotdog."

Catherine looked up at him and smiled then turned back to watch the street scattered with people.

"I would love a normal life," she said.

They walked the streets until eleven and then returned to Catherine's cottage. It took her less than ten minutes to throw her clothes into a suitcase, to look around for anything she might have missed, and to leave. Catherine drove her own car to the hotel, Luke following. She would call the owner of the cottage in the morning and settle her account with him. He would have wanted her to move out soon anyway; it was getting colder and as he had done with the green cottage next door, he would want to drain the pipes for the coming winter.

In their hotel room, they hugged one another closely, each knowing that in a few short hours, Luke would be gone.

Catherine looked around in the dimly lit room. "I won't be able to stay here for long," she said.

"I'll pay for the room," Luke began. "I want you to be safe and comfortable."

"It's not just the money," Catherine said, "it's the idea of being here without you. I think I could die of loneliness."

Luke held her tight. "You're not allowed to die of

anything," he said and then he added, "I've finally found my purpose in life – finding and loving *you*."

They watched the night sky with a glass of wine and then they slept, holding one another, until Luke left at four in the morning as planned.

Catherine wanted to cry when he left, but she smiled at him as he told her he loved her and he'd see her soon. Alone later, her eyes sought the solace offered by a darkened sky and then she drifted back to sleep.

With morning light, everything seemed darker. Luke was gone. She knew that this room simply wouldn't do. She dressed, packed her belongings and took them to the car. She would find a bed and breakfast.

Catherine drove into town, past her old cottage, glad to never step across that threshold again. She stopped at the café for coffee. As she reached for the door handle of the shop, Jack Stearn reached around her and pulled the door open for her.

"Looks like we both had the same idea at the same time," he said with a smile. "Will you join me for coffee?"

"Yes," she said. "I especially need the jolt this morning."

"Because of what I told you about the evil twins?"

"Not just that. Luke had to leave this morning."

Jack asked how she liked her coffee then said he'd be right back as he beckoned to a table in the corner.

Catherine sat down and unzipped her jacket. Jack placed two large cups down on the table then sat down facing her.

"Where was Luke off to?"

231

"He teaches college in Vermont."

"Vermont?" Jack said in a surprised voice. "That's a haul. How far up in the state did he need to drive?"

Catherine told Jack the name of the school and where it was located, near the Killington ski area.

"He seems like a devoted friend," he said to Catherine.

She smiled and nodded.

"So what are you doing out so early on this chilly morning, aside from having coffee with me?"

Catherine swallowed a few sips of hot coffee then placed the cup down. "I'm going to need to find a place to stay. Someplace inexpensive and clean; I can't deal with that cottage any longer."

Jack leaned forward. "I know just the place. My sister-in-law owns a small b and b here in town. Her rates at this time of year are very reasonable and the rooms are nice. She makes a good, hearty breakfast, too – none of that sweet roll and coffee stuff."

"That sounds perfect," Catherine said as she accepted a business card for Harbor Lights Bed and Breakfast.

"Is there anything new on Eric Bauer?" Catherine asked.

"Nothing much I can talk about. He's basically being dealt with now by immigration; he's a charming guy, a real Mr. Personality."

"It makes me wonder what Trini is like. Her photo shows a happy girl, a beautiful smile and twinkling eyes. How did she end up with brothers like Hans and Eric?"

"Different fathers, that's for certain."

"But all with the same last name," Catherine said.

"Apparently Helga Bauer never married."

When Jack left for work, Catherine sat and finished her coffee. She studied the business card for the bed and breakfast; she would go there after feeding the gulls.

Close to eleven when Catherine had stepped out of her car at the rocks, her cell phone rang. She smiled when she saw that it was Luke.

"Did you call to speak to the gulls?" she asked teasingly.

Luke laughed. "I figured you'd be there. How are they?"

"I'm sure they're fine. I just parked and am on my way over the rocks with two loaves of bread in my hands."

"I would have called earlier," he said, "but I ran into some road work on the highway and I was running late. I tried calling you; the cell doesn't always cooperate in the mountains and I hurried off to class. No coffee for you?" Luke asked.

"I had a cup with Jack Stearn."

"Should I be jealous?"

Catherine laughed and said, "I think you're safe."

"Anything new?"

Catherine made her way to their rocks and sat down, untying the loaves of bread. "Nothing new regarding Trini or the twins, but Jack gave me the address of a bed and breakfast. It's owned by his sister-in-law; I kind of like that the place is connected to someone I know and trust."

"I like that, too," Luke said. "This whole thing is a

little spooky. I wish we had some idea about why those guys wanted your sister. However, let's change the subject. I want you to know that with the sun brightly shining this morning, I held my kaleidoscope to the kitchen window and my eyes had a feast."

Catherine smiled as she tossed bread to the gulls. "I'm glad you like it, and I love my new blue shirt."

Luke groaned. "I hope that garment is being reserved for my eyes only," he said.

Catherine smiled. "No one else will ever know it exists."

"I hate to give up our conversation, but I have a class to teach in ten minutes. Will you call me later, or would you prefer that I call you?"

"I'll call you when I know about the bed and breakfast. I'll be able to tell you exactly where it is. I want you to be able to find me."

"Never doubt that I will find you," he said. "Promise me you'll be careful, Catherine. I know that having police training you're not a novice, but I still worry. Honestly, I'm glad those twins are out of the picture."

When the call ended and the last of the bread had been tossed in the air, the gulls dipping and screeching, Catherine scrambled to her feet and left the rocks. She felt the need to find the bed and breakfast and settle herself in. Once again, she drove past her cottage, shivered, then drove through town and took a right at the end of the road. She followed Jack's directions and looked for the street sign where Harbor Lights Bed and Breakfast was advertised as being one quarter of a mile away; Catherine drove and found a charming house

234

painted a pale blue with white trim. Flower boxes filled with varying shades of pink and red geraniums and stretches of hanging ivy graced each window.

Parking in a circular driveway before a large, double door, Catherine looked at what was about to become her new temporary home. As much as she felt relieved to be out of the cottage, it had become familiar, and now there was another change to endure. She shut down the engine and slid out of the car. She stood and looked at the front door, deciding to leave her belongings there until she registered. Before she could lock the car, a gray-haired woman in her sixties opened the door and smiled.

"Are you Jack's friend?" she asked.

Catherine returned the smile and walked toward the woman. "Yes," she said, "I'm Catherine."

The woman extended her hand. "I'm Jack's sister-in-law, Kate. Come in; let me show you the room. You'll have your own bathroom and you're free to use the parlor anytime you want. We're big on privacy here," she said as they walked into the house and toward the polished, dark-wood stairway.

The room shown to Catherine was large, bright, and beautifully decorated with flowered print wallpaper and off-white accessories.

"It's an old house," Kate said, "but we take good care of it and our guests."

"Thank you," Catherine said. "This is perfect."

Catherine walked downstairs and out to her car where she retrieved her suitcase and a small overnight bag. She looked at the sum of her present life – it was pathetic. She hauled the cases inside and up the stairs, leaving them on a bench at the foot of the bed.

She walked around the room and stopped at the double window overlooking a small yard with a rock wall; cascading bright yellow blooms and lush greenery spilled onto a manicured lawn. It was all undeniably pretty, and yet her heart and mind whirled with stress and loneliness.

Catherine walked downstairs and left the house, driving the mile into town. She parked her car in front of the pizza shop then walked to the café where she had her morning coffee. Placing an order for black tea and a tuna sandwich on toast, she sat at a corner table and made a call to Luke.

"Are you free?" she asked. "I hope I didn't catch you in class."

"I'm literally on my way out of the classroom, but let me call you back in about two minutes."

Within his estimated time, Luke's call came through. "Everything okay?" he asked.

"Everything's fine. I just moved into Harbor Lights Bed and Breakfast. The owner, Kate, is very friendly and the place is lovely. It's just missing one thing."

Luke laughed. "I hear you. I feel the same way about being here and my house. There's this one component missing. Where are you now? Did you go to our gulls?"

"I fed the gulls and right now I'm in the coffee shop having a sandwich and tea."

Luke sighed. "I wish I was there – or that you were here."

"Me too," she said.

"What's the agenda for this afternoon? I know

where you'll be this evening."

"I'm not sure what the afternoon will bring. I need to unpack and settle into my room, which is very nice, but other than that, I'm not sure. I can tell you one thing for certain: it's times like this that I miss not having a pet. When I get settled, I'm hitting a shelter and getting myself a compatible pair, a dog and a cat. It would be so much nicer to walk a dog around town than to go out on my own."

"Good, we'll get a dog and a cat, maybe two cats."

Catherine laughed. "Why two cats?"

"Well, when we go out with the dog, one cat on its own could be lonely."

Catherine laughed again. "Okay, two cats."

When their call ended, Catherine looked at the cold sandwich before her, took two bites, then drank her tea and left the café. She walked slowly, window-shopping, glancing every few seconds to the street, her eyes in the endless search. At one point she looked to a shop window where she caught the reflection of a girl getting into a car with a male driver across the street. She had blonde hair and the body of a young woman. Catherine turned and stared at the car, then walked quickly to her own vehicle.

She moved in behind the wheel, started the engine, and slowly, cautiously, followed the car. They drove for several miles with Catherine's heart pounding and her mind wondering how far this pair might travel. At a red light, Catherine was immediately in back of them and watched, as it seemed they might have been arguing. *Could that be Trini?* She followed behind as the light turned green and then they pulled into a fast food restaurant. Catherine pulled into the parking lot but stayed a distance away. Within moments, the two exited the car and Catherine sighed as she sat back in her seat. The blonde was young, she was pretty, but she was not Trini.

Catherine rubbed her eyes and wasn't sure how she felt. If this girl had been her sister, how would she have handled the situation? She had already made a note of the license plate and model of car, but what would justify a call to the police? She was both disappointed and relieved with the outcome.

When the pair had gone into the busy establishment, Catherine sat for a few moments then drove out of the parking lot and onto the highway back toward the beach. She noted the town's name on a historic sign and realized she had driven about thirty miles. As she drove, her cell phone rang and she was surprised to see that the number was Luke's.

"Hi," she said, "don't you have a class you're supposed to be teaching?"

"There was an adjustment – I'm actually on my way to you."

Catherine felt bewildered. "Why? I mean, I can't wait to see you, but what made this possible?"

"Catherine, where are you?"

"I'm about thirty miles from the beach. I saw someone who looked like Trini. I followed them. It wasn't Trini, but of course, I needed to know."

"Catherine," he said in a serious tone, "please go back to the bed and breakfast. I'll be there in about three hours."

"Luke, what's wrong? Are you okay? Where are

you?"

"I just passed through Hooksett. Catherine, please wait for me at the b and b."

"Can't you tell me what's going on?"

"We'll talk when I get there. I'll see you soon."

Catherine didn't understand what would bring Luke back to Rhode Island on a school day. The thought of what might propel him to her so suddenly caused her to feel frightened and confused.

"Luke," she said in a half-strangled voice before their call ended, "I have no idea what's going on, but I love you. I love you."

She could hear Luke exhale a deep breath. "I love you, too," he said.

Catherine wiped away a stray tear. She did not understand why Luke was on his way back to Rhode Island, but it was obvious that something was wrong. Could he have lost his position? She thought, too, of how easy it was to say the words she had never said to another: *I love you.*

Forty minutes later when she arrived back at Harbor Lights, Kate Stearn was at the door to greet her. The woman's kind face was somber.

"Come in, Dear," she said. "I've just made tea. Come and have a cup with me."

Catherine hesitated then began to walk with Kate, feeling a twist in her stomach while experiencing her life in slow motion. Catherine reached out and put her arm on Kate's as they walked into the kitchen.

"Did something happen to Jack?" she asked.

"Jack is fine," Kate said and then she gestured for Catherine to sit down at the table. The woman spoke so fast about the day: the coming cold, the need for tea, getting the house ready to accommodate a convention in another month, Catherine had no time to think or to speak. The tea was good, hot and soothing.

After more than an hour in Kate's kitchen, Catherine finished the last of her tea and took the cup to the sink.

"I think I'll go up to my room and change clothes," she said with a smile. "Luke is coming; he should be here soon."

She was thinking that she should explain about Luke, but she didn't know what to say and Kate didn't ask. Catherine thanked Kate for the tea and went up to her room where suitcases sat unpacked. She looked in the mirror and decided she needed to brush her hair and find something other than jeans and a jersey to welcome Luke back, whatever the reason. She took a pair of chino pants from her suitcase and then a blouse in deep blue. They weren't perfectly smooth, but they would do. She slipped out of her jeans and jersey, brushed her hair then dressed, applying just a touch of color to her lips.

At first she walked to the window and looked out to the small yard and then she glanced further down the street where two neighbors had parked boats in their driveways. The area was tight but well-kept – there was a sense of community; it reminded her of where she grew up.

Catherine walked over to her bed and sat down. She thought about unpacking her suitcases, but felt restless waiting and wondering about Luke. She looked at her watch. By his calculations, he could be there any moment.

"Catherine?" she heard his voice and the light knock at the door.

Anxious, but thrilled to have him back, she opened the door wide. Her smile vanished as she saw that Jack Stearn was standing next to Luke. They stepped into her room and she moved aside, in awe of the two serious faces.

They looked at her. Catherine began to shiver. "What's going on?" she said in a soft voice.

"Sit down, Sweetheart," Luke suggested and gestured toward the bed.

Catherine shook her head and remained standing. "Tell me," she said. "Just tell me."

Luke and Jack looked at one another.

"We found your sister," Jack said as his eyes moved from Catherine's beautiful face to the floor. "I thought it best for Luke to be here."

Catherine stood motionless, not aware of her own shallow breaths. "What do you mean?" she finally said, her stare going to Jack's grim expression.

He looked at her. "I'm sorry, Catherine. Trini is dead."

Catherine literally bent in half, like a rag doll, and then she went down to the floor on her knees, sobbing. Luke knelt down on one knee and held her.

"I'm sorry, Sweetheart," he said with his lips to her hair. "I'm so sorry."

Between gasps for breath and sobs, she asked, "How? When did this happen? Where is she?"

Luke looked up at Jack Stearn as Catherine looked incredulously at the detective.

241

Jack shook his head. "It happened several days ago. We just found her body."

"Who did this? Where did it happen? How did she die?" The questions ran like a babbling brook through her mind and heart. It couldn't be. Not Trini. Not the sister she longed to know.

Jack was unusually silent for several minutes before he told Catherine that Trini had been taken by the coroner – she was in the city morgue.

"Where was she?" Catherine asked with tears and sobs saturating her words. "Where had she been all that time I was searching for her?"

Luke looked at Jack and again, Jack shook his head. "She was in the green cottage next to yours," he said.

Catherine buried her head in Luke's arms and agonizingly cried. "No," she said, "no."

"Maybe," Jack began, "it would be best if we let Catherine have some rest. We can continue this later."

"*No*," she half screamed. "No. I want to know everything, every single detail. Who did this? Her twin brothers were next to me. Are you telling me that she was there, that they had her all the time? They did this? Why was she in the cottage next to mine? How was she found?"

Jack shifted his weight from one foot to the other, his hands clutched at the buttons of his overcoat. "The landlord was cleaning the interior of your cottage and the green one for winter preparations. That's when she was found. She was bound and left, Catherine. It looks like she might have died of dehydration. We really don't know yet."

Catherine sobbed. "She was there and I had no idea. I was out looking for her every day and she was right there - *right there*." Catherine covered her eyes and the stream of tears spilled onto her slim fingers.

Luke tightened his grasp; there were no words to console her.

"Are you sure? Are you positive it was Trini?" Catherine looked at Jack and pleaded for another answer.

"We're sure," he said softly.

"Catherine," Luke said as he held her close to him, "we'll talk more about this later. I promise, we're not sweeping this under a rug, we're not letting go of your devotion to Trini. Right now, you've had enough."

Luke urged Catherine to stand and walk to the bed. She lay down in a fetal position and he gently covered her with a quilt.

Jack looked at Luke and nodded. "We'll talk more later. Try to get her to rest a bit," he spoke low. "This has been a hell of a blow to her. I'll be at the station if she wants to see me. I have more to tell her, but this isn't the time."

"What if she wants to see her sister's body?" Luke asked softly at the door.

"I wouldn't advise it, but if that's what she wants, maybe tomorrow. There's an autopsy going on later today."

Luke nodded and Jack turned toward the door. The two men did not say goodbye. They parted in silence, as death demands.

When Jack left and the door was closed, Luke walked back toward the bed and thought that Catherine was asleep.

"Luke," she whispered weakly, "don't leave me."

He sat down on the edge of the bed and took her hand. "Never," he said firmly. After a few moments, Luke stretched out beside her, his arms around her, the two of them molded together.

Catherine slept for several hours and was so still that Luke listened for her soundless breathing. When she woke after midnight, Luke had coffee for her brought to the room by Kate. Catherine rejected it at first, but with Luke's urging, she accepted a cup and sipped at its warmth as she sat up against the pillows.

"Why?" she asked tearfully. "Why, Luke, why?"

Luke had no answers. He shook his head and looked out to the dark beyond the window, then back to Catherine's tear-filled eyes. "I wish I had answers, Sweetheart. I know you're heartbroken. I know."

When he saw that Catherine was shaking with sobs again, he moved quickly to place the coffee cup on the bedside table. He sat down on the bed and held her, her face buried in his shoulder where darkness embraced her eyes keeping her from the grim reality light allowed in.

"I'm so sorry, Darling," he whispered against her hair.

The twenty-four hours that followed left Catherine feeling numb and forlorn. She wanted to see Trini. For one time, even in death, she wanted to see her, to speak the words that they were sisters and that she loved her. She wanted to touch her blonde hair, just for a moment.

"What was she wearing when you brought her here?" she asked softly of the medical examiner.

The elderly man peered over his glasses at Catherine's sad face. "Jeans, a white t-shirt and a gray button-front sweater."

Catherine closed her eyes and covered her mouth. It had been her sister at the window of the cottage, her palm against the pane.

Catherine looked at the youthful face, so still. She walked close to where her young body stretched out beneath a plain white sheet and gently touched the girl's forehead, as if to wake her. Then she touched the thick braid to Trini's left side. Her hair was like silk, fastened with a simple rubber band.

"I have something I want her to have," she robotically murmured. "I want it to go with her."

Luke lowered his head and remembered the red sweater purchased at the Providence Mall. He would see to it that Trini had her gift.

"A small notebook, a diary of sorts, was found with your sister. It may," the examiner said, "be something you'll be able to have – talk to Jack Stearn about it."

Catherine's heart quickened with the thought of the smallest chance to know her sister through written words. She looked from the medical examiner to Luke, tears streaming from her eyes.

"We'll talk to Jack," Luke said reassuringly.

Chapter Sixteen

That day would never be forgotten and, in fact, would be cherished for the opportunity to see, to touch Trini. Shattered with grief, Catherine could not let go. She did not feel comfort in rest or prayer. She felt the need to know more, to have this loss explained to her. She would ask the question over and over, *why?* Why did her sister die?

With determination and strength she didn't know she possessed, Catherine, with Luke at her side, went to Jack Stearn's office in the police station. When he saw her standing before him, Jack ran his fingers through his sparse gray hair and looked at the young woman's mournful expression.

"Come and sit down, Catherine," he invited and gestured toward two chairs opposite his own. Luke urged Catherine to one as he took the other.

"The medical examiner said you might have a notebook, something Catherine might see or have," Luke said.

Without a word, Jack reached into his desk and brought out a small leather-bound journal in a shade of dusty blue. He looked at it then handed it to Catherine.

"It's yours," he said. "There is nothing there for evidence concerning her troubles. It's mostly the thoughts and dreams of a young girl."

Catherine touched the supple cover. Trini's hands had held that little book, the story of her brief life. She turned it over and over, ran her forefinger along the golden edges of the inch-thick collection of pages. She opened it to the first page and saw the name in cursive black ink, Trinity Bauer. Catherine swallowed back tears. She could not look further there, in that sterile police environment. She did not know where or when she would be able to open that book, revealing the thoughts of a young girl who seemed to have been abandoned and taunted by circumstance.

Catherine shielded the small journal between her slim hands and rested them in her lap, staring at the blue leather.

"I have more for you, Catherine," Jack said. "It's in the safe at a jeweler's just now, but I should be able to get it for you tomorrow. It's the necklace."

Catherine looked up at Jack. "The one I brought here to the station?"

Jack nodded. "We discovered through a nanny friend of your sister's, a nice little Irish girl, that the necklace has quite a story. Do you want to hear it now or would you prefer to wait another day or two?"

"Please tell me," she said.

Jack sat back in his chair. "During the time that your father and Helga were dating, they went to a street fair where Helga saw and liked the necklace. Your father bought it for her for around five dollars. No one knew its worth. When Helga returned to Germany, someone there recognized the necklace as being a Corini original, a very pricey piece of jewelry. Helga had it appraised and discovered it was worth a small

247

fortune. Apparently the twins got wind of the value and wanted it. Helga said it was bought by Trini's father and it was to be hers. That's when the evil pair began their hunt, after Trini came here to be a nanny.

"When the twins caught up with their sister, they kidnapped her, kept her in that little cottage next to yours. The necklace was to be delivered to them as ransom. As you know," he said, "it was left on your doorstep. Now we know that was a mistake. The person who delivered it had the wrong cottage. The twins were furious. Before they left the cottage for good, they tied your sister to a chair, taped her mouth and left her. She died of dehydration."

Catherine covered her face in horror.

"It's worth a lot of money, Catherine. In that little book you have there, Trini tells of her wish, and the wish of her mother, that in the event of their demise, the necklace should go to you. She knew you existed, Catherine. You can read it for yourself; she knew she had a sister. She didn't know your name or where you were, but she was hoping someday to find you. She was a good girl."

Catherine was stunned. "I always felt that she was," she whispered.

Jack looked at Luke and then again at Catherine. "That necklace has been appraised for about eight-hundred thousand dollars. The appraiser has a Corini collector in mind and knows he can guarantee you at least that much, maybe more if you're interested in selling."

Catherine did not speak. Without a doubt, she would sell the necklace, which was riddled with harsh memories and inadvertently caused her sister's death.

After Trini's burial in a beachside cemetery, Catherine and Luke sat on their rocks tossing bread to the gulls. Luke glanced at Catherine's beautiful face, somber with sadness.

"We'll come back here often," he said. "We have a mission – to feed the gulls and to tend to Trini's grave. We won't forget what we lost, and we won't neglect what we found here."

Catherine was silent.

"Sometime soon," he said, "I'd like to take you to meet my Aunt Ruthie and my dad. You'll like them."

Catherine looked at Luke. "How are we going to explain our relationship to Ruthie?"

Luke shook his head and smiled. "She already knows."

Catherine looked at Luke with questions in her expression.

"It seems that months ago she called my old parish. They told her. She was patiently waiting for *me* to tell her. She's okay; she wants to meet you."

Catherine nodded. The life she'd been living seemed to be a blur, and yet the future felt crystal clear.

"I know we'll need to come back in a week or two to deal with your apartment, but for now, are we ready to head for Vermont?" he asked. "We can grab a coffee for the road."

"I'm ready to go *anywhere* with you, Luke. But

before we go, I need you to know about an idea I've had. I want to use some of the money from the sale of the necklace to invest in a small bookstore near the college. I have chosen a name for it – *Trinity Books*, in honor of my sister and the life you chose as a young man. Without having made that choice, you might have moved in another direction – and without my search for Trini, we might never have met."

Luke hugged Catherine to his side, the early autumn winds pulling at their light jackets and Catherine's long hair.

"I feel as if meeting you was the birth of me," he said.

They stood, glancing out to the deep green of the ocean and then to the gulls on the rocks below. They looked at one another then pressed their foreheads together. Catherine knew that Luke was still wondering, as was she, where the seagulls found rest and resolve from determined wind and penetrating cold.

"I think we should come back during February vacation and give these guys a hearty feeding," he said. "Bread may not sustain them for more than a day, but I think it gives them hope. Survival needs hope."

Catherine nodded and smiled as she wrapped her arms around Luke's waist and then they turned toward his car and a future filled with peace and promise.

> *Whatever our souls are made of,*
> *his and mine are the same.*
> ~Emily Bronte

www.ingramcontent.com/pod-product-compliance
Lightning Source LLC
Chambersburg PA
CBHW070815180626
46818CB00001B/271